# Independent Brake

## A Dominion Falls Novel

## Sarah Cass

**Historical Western Romance**

**A Divine Roses Ink Book**
Historical Western Romance
First E-book Publication: December 2014
Second E-book Publication: May 2018
First Print Publication: May 2018

Independent Brake: A Dominion Falls Novel
Copyright © 2014 Sarah Cass

Cover design by Sarah Cass
Edited by Megan Koenen
Proofread by Mary Terrani

**PUBLISHER**
**Divine Roses Ink**
http://www.divinerosesink.com

# Other Books in
# The Dominion Falls Series

Changing Tracks
Derailed
Dark Territory
Runaway Train
Home Signal
Red Zone

# Coming Soon in
# The Dominion Falls Series

Dust Raiser
Blizzard Lights
Dead Man's Switch
Bird Cage
A Highball Arrangement
Douse the Glim
Blood
Grave Digger
Bad Order

# Books by Sarah Cass

**The Tribe Series**

The Tribe

The Wolf

The Chief

The Raven

**The Lake Point Series**

Santa, Maybe

Deep-Fried Sweethearts

Stalled Independence

Witch Way

A Thorough Thanksgiving

Eve's New Year

Heartstrings & Hockey Pucks

Luck of the Cowgirl

Stars, Stripes & Motorbikes

Free Falling

Love for Hire

Haunted Hearts

**Stand Alone Novels**

Masked Hearts

Leap

# Dedication

To my husband, my champion.
I know you didn't understand at first,
But you still supported me.
Now you push me to write,
And I thank you for all of it.

Oh yeah, and I guess for the kids too. ;)

# Runaway

Katherine's father stepped into her room after the slightest of knocks. His thinning red hair shimmered in the sunlight. The grin he wore was contagious. "Are you ready, Katherine?"

"Of course I am." Katherine leapt from her bed with an enthusiasm that would have disappointed her mother thoroughly. After all, a proper society lady behaved with decorum always. Too bad Katherine had such trouble following the rules of society. She knew her father wouldn't mind, he had been the one teasing her mercilessly for weeks over her surprise. She smoothed out the full width of her skirts and spun. "Am I dressed appropriately?"

"Hmm." He took her hand and spun her as if they were about to begin a waltz. "You might be a little fancy, but that is the norm for us, is it not?"

"It is now." Katherine agreed. Since her sister, Martha's, embarrassing turn of a pregnancy out of wedlock to an Indian, and their subsequent secret marriage while she was engaged to the delightful Mr. Schaffer; Katherine's mother had become far more obsessed with asserting their position in Dominion Falls, Colorado.

The result had been a new wardrobe full of the latest fashions, uncomfortable corsets and ungainly hoops; and frequent trips to Denver which left Katherine utterly bored with society, as well as the proper young gentlemen with whom her mother had been encouraging her to get acquainted. At fifteen, Katherine might've been the age to consider proper marriage, but the thought had never appealed to her. Perhaps it was growing up her whole life among miners, but she thought there might be more fun in life than being a proper wife.

"I certainly didn't mean to upset you." Her father chucked his finger under her chin. "This is supposed to be a surprise, not a funeral."

"Sorry. So long as my surprise isn't us moving to Denver, I'm certain I'll love it."

For a moment her father's smile seemed to falter, but the moment was so brief she dismissed it as her overactive imagination. He held out his arm to her. "You will have to close your eyes, but I'll let you get all the way down the stairs first."

"The surprise requires me to close my eyes?" She couldn't stop her excited little hop to grab his arm. "That means it's definitely a big one. What have you gotten for me, father?"

"Something that has set in your mother's mind I spoil you too much."

Katherine giggled at his wink and stepped down the steps with him as if light as a feather. At least her excitement kept her from what her mother described as unladylike stomping down the stairs, heaven forbid she raced as she once had when she was small. "She never complained when I was a child."

"Life was different then, you know that. This mining camp and our business has grown to such that we can't be who we were then."

"I don't see why not. People liked us then. Now they look at me different."

At the bottom of the stairs, he paused. A small frown tugged his smile away. "How so? The men aren't…"

When her father's voice trailed off, Katherine raised her eyebrows. "The men aren't what, Father? I just mean they look at me like they do mother. My old friends, the men that used to be real nice all treat me like I think I'm better than them."

"Oh." His shoulders sagged and he exhaled a breath so big she wondered if he'd been holding it. "I see. Well, that's of no consequence at the moment. You just keep being you and they'll see you haven't changed, Katherine."

"Easier said than done. Now what about my surprise?" She hopped up on her toes and bounced. "Can I see it now? Can I?"

"Close your eyes." Her father's warm chuckle filled the hallway even as she obliged him and his visage disappeared behind her eyelids. His warm grasp on her arm guided her down the hall.

"How far are you going to take me? You're torturing me this way." Katherine tried to put just enough whine into her voice and puffed out her lip just enough to try to guilt a clue from him. All she got in response was more laughter.

"You aren't being tortured. You're just impatient. We're almost there. Hold on. We should stop here for a moment." When her father stopped her, there was a small bustling of petticoats nearby before a cloak was draped over her shoulders.

"My cloak? My surprise is outside?" The typically cold winter of Dominion Falls had hit as early as it ever did. Snow blanketed most of the town, and all of their yard and the surrounding woods in a beautiful coat of white.

"Very astute of you. Here we go." The door opened with a blast of cool air and her father guided her outside.

The cold tickled her nose and she willingly leaned against him when he wrapped his arm around her shoulder. A whinny caught her ears on a blast of wind and without permission she opened her eyes. Not that it mattered she'd beat him to the punch; she'd been left speechless by what she found.

Off at the far end of the yard a brilliant white horse as clean as the snow shook its head out. Her father whistled in her ear and the horse whinnied in response before it started to run toward them.

"I'd tell you that you can open your eyes now, but I see you already have. What do you think, Katherine? You were complaining about the brown being too old for you."

"I—I just—oh, she's beautiful father! Is she really mine?" Katherine burst from her father's hold to run toward the fence that bordered the paddock. The horse slowed down nearby and ambled toward her and the carrot she dug out of the bag her father held out to her. "I thought you said we didn't need another horse."

"I did, but I saw this one for sale in Pueblo. She was wild as the day is long, but I thought that would be better suited for your equally fiery personality. I've had her fully broken and trained for you, with just a little bit of wild left."

She grinned when the horse took the carrot from her hand. With a small sigh she rubbed her hand along the velvet nose. "I'll call her Powder."

"Like a powder keg. A fitting name."

"Thank you." Katherine spun and clasped her father in the tightest hug she possibly could. "She's the most beautiful horse there ever was."

"You're welcome." He squeezed her shoulder when they parted. "Why don't you take a few minutes to get to know her? You and I can go for a ride after supper."

"All right." She smiled bright even as she caught sight of her mother on the porch. When her father moved to join her mother, she turned back to Powder. She fed Powder another carrot and spoke low. "There are no presents without reason, Powder. I just don't know what you mean."

She glanced at the porch and the quiet debate going on between her parents. Her mother's triumphant nod of her head before she headed back inside didn't ease Katherine's concern. Even worse was the painful attempt at a bright smile her father made before he waved and followed her mother.

"I guess hoping you are just because the brown is getting old is too much to ask, isn't it, Powder?"

The horse nudged her almost off the fence as it tried to get into the bag of carrots.

"You aren't helpful. Not at all." Katherine chuckled and dug out another carrot to feed to the horse. "But you are beautiful. And mine."

* * * *

"Afternoon, Miss Daugherty." Gilbert Hamm tipped his hat with a broad gap-toothed smile. "Fine horse you got there. She new?"

"Sure is, Mr. Hamm." Katherine leaned down to pat Powder's neck. "It's our first time out. Thought I'd swing by the library today and see if Mother ordered anything new."

"Stage ain't been in for weeks. They'd best get here before next snow fall or the town'll be hurtin'." Mr. Hamm lifted his hat to scratch the top of his balding head. "Turners are 'bout out of supplies. The store's got empty shelves first time in my memory."

"Kelly has empty shelves?" Katherine flinched at the slip in decorum that would have won a scolding from her mother.

Then again, her mother wasn't anywhere around. She leaned down. "Hammy. What about the stash?"

Hammy hop-stepped closer to the horse and winked. "I checked. Kelly's still got a good supply of syrup from last year's tapping hidden in the cellar. We're good for candy long as the snow falls."

"Good." For years whenever the weather was cold Katherine had slipped off to Kelly's to make candy using the snow and warm syrup. Hammy had been the sponsor of the activity as he supplied much of the syrup off his own gold claim. It was no wonder the man rarely brought back gold. She smiled and straightened. "Then mayhap I'll see you tomorrow when the snow is fresh."

"I'll let Kelly and Cora know. That young'un of theirs is just the right age to start making his own."

"Arthur'll be four any day now. High time he joined us." Katherine nodded. "I'll see you then."

Hammy waved as she urged Powder on down the road. Where just weeks ago hammers and saws had rang through the muddy streets silence now lingered. Buildings had been abandoned in a series of heavy snows that left piles of lumber still buried today.

Vendors crowded every inch of the street around the abandoned building projects. Tents lined the next street over behind the skeletal signs of the attempts of the large camp to become a town.

Katherine knew every one of the vendors, her parents had made sure to know all of the camps members as they joined, until recently. They'd stopped meeting the stages after Martha's embarrassing folly. Many things had changed since that travesty.

A sharp whistle pulled Katherine out of her own thoughts, and she tugged the reins on instinct. The moment she realized the culprit behind the whistle was Cole Mitchell she wished she hadn't stopped. The man always left her flustered and beside herself. When she'd first started to notice boys, both Cole and her sister's fiancé, David, had captured her imaginings.

Nowadays David was long gone, but in recent months Cole had begun to speak directly to her on regular occasions. It infuriated her mother, and gave Katherine a disturbing, secret little thrill. Rumors of how well-pleased Cole's women of ill-repute were kept flew fast and easy in a camp like this.

Cole was nearly seven years older than her, and had come to town just two years before. The few proper women in town told tales he took in whores young as fourteen, but Katherine had met many of the whores and doubted any were below eighteen. She also suspected Cole helped along any rumors he could.

Either way, the man was a sight that turned many a lady's head, proper or no. To have such a man, a rake, a letch, whatever he may be, pay Katherine any mind had its own flattery. She rather enjoyed the attention, and didn't discourage it as much as she likely should considering his sort of business.

Ashamed that such thoughts should dare to cross her mind, Katherine tried to again reclaim her wits as Cole stopped just near her foot. "May I assist you in some way, Mr. Mitchell?"

"Fine looking horse ya got there." Cole's lip curved into a knowing smirk. "You enjoying your bribe?"

Heat rushed to her cheeks and she narrowed her eyes. "I beg your pardon?"

"Blizzard. She's a bribe with a hell of a price tag. You did know that, didn't ya?"

"Blizzard?"

"The horse. That was her name when I was training her. Why, what did ya name her?" He chuckled. "Let me guess. Somethin' real pretty like Snowy or Princess."

Her short, angry huffs of breath formed into steam in the cold air and she lifted her chin to hide the way she had to blink back her tears. Rather than tell him what she'd named the horse she spoke through her clenched jaw. "*You* trained her?"

"Of course. Who else is gonna train a horse in this camp? Especially a wild one like this beast was." He rubbed the horse's flank and nodded. "I knew she was going to you, though, so I kept a little wild in her. I think ya got some wild in you that ain't been unleashed yet too."

"I think you're speaking far too inappropriately."

"Fifteen is the right age. Can't tell ya how many women find themselves then. Got three girls now that are near-sixteen. Besides, your parents are marrying you off at fifteen. Guess it ain't so inappropriate after all."

"I am not a whore, nor will I be." She drew up straight, trying to process what he'd said. "And my parents aren't marrying me off so young."

"It ain't so young. And yeah, they are." He shrugged. "What do ya think the horse is for?"

Katherine pondered the quiet conversation she'd witnessed back at the house. The timing of Powder's arrival didn't make her a gift for birthday or Christmas. The talk of going to Denver permanently, and the courting she'd been forced to take part in when they did visit.

"So your Pa didn't tell you yet." Cole clicked his tongue and shook his head. "Such a shame too. Gonna waste your whole life on a marriage of convenience."

"What do you know of marriage anyhow?" Katherine tried to put venom into her tone, but instead it trembled dangerously close to tears. "My parents' marriage is good."

"I know more'n you'd think, and your parents eloped. Heard from your Pa himself, they liked each other. You got a guy you like, Kathy?"

"My name is Katherine."

"I like Kathy. Suits ya better."

On Katherine's left a door slammed open. Her sister, Martha, stormed into the street. Her light brown hair had begun to gray already after the stresses of the past two years. It flew out of her bun in unruly strands as she rushed toward Katherine and Cole. "Cole Mitchell, you get on away from her! Katherine Marie Daugherty, what do you think you're doing speaking to the likes of him?"

"This is all *your* fault, Martha." Katherine spat the words before she could think too hard on what she was saying. "And I have always spoken to Mr. Mitchell. It's polite."

"Katherine! How is it my fault you're speaking with a man that keeps loose women. You know he only wants to make you one. I've heard him saying it." Martha narrowed her eyes at the man who only grinned in response.

"I'd bet anything he's said such things because you eavesdrop and you are impossible." Katherine swung out of her saddle and dropped right down onto the frozen street to meet her older sister's angry stance with one of her own. "All of this is your fault. The horse, the arranged marriage. All because you couldn't keep your legs together around a damned red man."

"Katherine!" Martha's jaw dropped, and Cole's laughter rang through the street, drawing more attention their way. "You'd best watch your—"

"I will not! You are the cause for my whole life changing." Tears burned at the back of Katherine's eyes as the full weight of what Cole suggested hit her. To be married off to a virtual stranger, to lose even more of the life she loved here in Dominion Falls. It was more than she could take, and she snapped. "Because of you, everything is changing. Don't you dare tell me to be silent because it's all your fault. You left a good man to be a whore to a red man—"

Katherine's cheek stung seconds before she registered Martha had slapped her. She clasped her hand over the sore cheek and stared at Martha.

"Hey now." Cole stepped out from under Powder's neck and positioned himself in front of Katherine. "Don't go beatin' your sister for bein' honest."

"I'll have you know," Martha began, "that she is a child. She shouldn't be saying such things when she knows nothing about them."

"She's no child. Your parents are gonna have her wed before the end of the year if they can, just so she don't mix with riff raff. And she's got a point. Wouldna happened if you hadn't taken up with an Injun."

"Lewis is emancipated." Martha all but hissed, her hand twitching like she was going to slap him too. "Practically white."

"Only with his paint on, Martha. Ain't no way he's ever gonna be one of us."

Katherine backed up, but bumped into Powder. Married by the end of the year? That was barely over two months away. It couldn't be. She spun and gripped the pommel to lift herself back into the saddle. Before she got far, she was lifted the rest of the way and Cole slapped Powder's flank over Martha's protests.

Without time for even a nod of gratitude in Cole's direction, Katherine leaned over and let Powder race her out of town toward the small settlement of homes starting to sprout up north of town. She didn't dare go too far for fear of Indians, but she would run until she found somewhere to hole up and think.

She couldn't get married. Not now. Not in Denver.

She'd barely begun to live.

* * * *

Katherine sat cross-legged on her bed, picking at a loose thread in the quilt her mother had made ages ago when she still did such menial tasks. The quilt was now as worn as Katherine's hope, but a stubborn flame of rebellion flared in her belly.

There was no good reason to be treated this way. She wasn't like Martha, she never had been, and yet her parents were going to do everything in their power to change the course of her fate. She tried to slouch and pout, but her corset refused her even that bit of bend.

With a wince, she adjusted the confounded contraption and readjusted the way she sat instead. A knock at the door made her push aside her attempts to plan a way out of her current situation.

"Katherine. It's time for supper." Her mother didn't bother to open the door. Propriety stood that Katherine should join them.

"I'm not hungry." Childish, most likely, but right then Katherine didn't want to face her parents. Of course, her refusal would probably bring about that very situation.

"I didn't ask if you were hungry." The door opened and Lillian stepped into the room with her unhappiest of expressions. "I stated that supper was ready, which means you'll join us."

"And I told you, I'm not hungry. I don't wish to dine with you." Katherine turned her back on her mother and rose to her feet.

"Katherine. I won't tolerate such behavior. I am still your mother, and you will do as I say."

"You're treating me like a child." Katherine lifted her chin and took a few steps closer to the window. "And yet you expect me to be wed before the end of the year."

For a moment the silence lingered, and confirmed every rumor. Her mother got her wits about her fast enough, though. "We were hoping to discuss our plans over supper."

"Well we're discussing them now." Katherine turned to face her mother. "To whom have you decided to sell me?"

"You aren't being sold. Don't be so ridiculous." Her mother took one step as if to storm through the room as she once had when upset. Instead, she gathered herself up all proper again. "We want to be sure you are cared for and want for nothing."

"Who, Mother?"

"Benjamin Lawson."

The last bit of hope for a good future she'd held onto sputtered and died. Her heart shriveled. Like a stone it dropped into a sick pit in the bottom of her stomach. Of all the suitors her parents had allowed courtship with, Benjamin was the most boring, mind-numbing rotten apple of the lot.

"He's well-to-do. You'll have your home to run, and time for leisure. Your children will be set for their lives."

"Leisure? I don't want to tea with the women I've met there. Their lives are boring. There is no color, there is no life."

"There is life everywhere in the city. Far better than the chaos and crass amusement those around here partake in. They survive on liquor and whores. There are more men than women and they are nothing like men we should associate with."

"They're the men you associated with for years. You played cards with Hammy."

"It's Mr. Hamm," her mother corrected with snap of her fingers. "I'll have you remember your place."

"I'm sorry; it's so easy to forget when just two years ago I was able to associate with any of these people freely. Before you sequestered us in this house away from the riff raff you once called friends."

Her mother's eyes widened and her nostrils flared before she folded her hands across her stomach. "What's done is done, Katherine. Mr. Lawson is a good match."

"For you and Father. But what of me? What of love?"

"Love has little place—"

"It had *every* place for you and father! You eloped with him." Katherine turned and planted her palms against the cold window, and quickly followed the action up with her forehead in an attempt to cool herself and her temper.

She felt no triumph over her mother's surprised silence, only her own sense of defeat. Out in the paddock Powder sprinted away from the stable hand trying to get her into the stable as the first snowflakes drifted down.

Her soft sigh left a cloud of steam on the window, blurring the image as her joy was now fogged in oppression. "I am not Martha."

"Of course you aren't. We've ensured—"

"No. I wasn't Martha before you began this pursuit to make us the toast of Denver society. You didn't have to sell me into this life to keep me from the life Martha chose."

"Again, we haven't sold you. Don't make this out to be like slavery. You haven't the faintest idea what—"

"You offered my hand to the man with the greatest bank account. You expect me to be a prim and proper wife which, until Martha took up with an Indian, you never were. I remember what it was like before, Mother. While you did try to improve this camp with a library and a church, you weren't this person in front of me dictating my life."

"We all have choices to make. I'm sorry you don't like all of mine, but there is nothing to be done now. You'll see when you're old enough to understand and have children of your own. This is what's best."

"And when you're old and gray sitting around with nothing but one daughter married to an Indian and no grandchildren, you'll see this was the worst choice you made. I won't give him children. I don't even want his slimy hands touching me."

"Katherine Marie, proper women don't speak of such things!"

Katherine closed her eyes and bit her lips to cover her rising chuckle. Until this moment she'd never realized how much she didn't want to be a proper anything. She took a deep breath and gathered her calm. Perhaps if she gave in, for now, her mother would let her guard down and Katherine could plan. Plan what, she didn't know, but she knew she had to plan something. "When do you plan to leave for Denver?"

"Two weeks. Your father has business to wrap up. His new foreman is doing well, so we see little reason to linger for the worst of the snows."

"What about the lack of a stagecoach? Mr. Hamm says none has been around for three weeks."

"We'll have transportation. Never you mind that. Now chin up, join us for supper."

Katherine straightened up and tugged her bodice taught across her corset. First course of action would be to belligerently agree to the plan. Then she had to find someone to assist her. She had no idea what to do or where to go, but she knew she couldn't go to Denver.

A prim and proper life would never suit her. She had too much of Dominion Falls in her heart and spirit. One way or the other she would find a way to get out and figure out what she was meant for.

Cole was right about one thing.

No longer would she be a child.

\* \* \* \*

Poor Hammy.

He'd fought her tooth and nail. Katherine had been forced to make promises and swear on nothing short of a bible to get him to agree to help her. Between swearing she wasn't turning herself in to become a soiled dove and that she wouldn't cave to Cole's considerable charms, she only prayed she wouldn't let the sweet old Mr. Hamm down.

Certainly, the last thing in her plans was to be a whore.

No, she had a tiny bit of a plan to get out of Dominion Falls, but she'd need help. Anyone else in town would tell her parents. After all, her parents owned most of the camp's land and anyone with a vested interest tended to kowtow.

Not Cole.

It was risky to put any trust in a man in his business, but she had little choice.

The back door of the saloon cracked open. Hammy stepped outside, the same displeased furrow in his brow as when he'd gone in the front. For some reason Cole liked Hammy more than most of the men in town, and gave him alone the freedom to disturb him before business hours.

Katherine ducked through the fence of Cole's corral and ran toward the gate. "Well?"

"He's comin'." Hammy's harsh whisper cut through the cold wind. He paused at the gate and pulled it open when she got close. "I don't like this. Not one bit. He seemed real eager to see ya."

"It'll be fine, Hammy. You'll see."

Movement in the door Hammy had left open pulled Katherine's attention away. Cole's tall frame filled the doorway before he slipped outside. Despite the temperatures the man didn't wear a coat; only boots, trousers, and a unionsuit that left little to her young mind's imaginings.

Katherine ducked her head to hide the heat of her blush and pulled her muffler further up her face. At the very least the cold gave her an excuse for red cheeks. Out of the corner of her eye she noticed Hammy step a respectable few feet away, but still close enough to hear everything.

"What's so important ya had to wake me so damn early?" Cole didn't even shiver when he leaned on the fence next to her.

"I need some help and there's no one else in town I can ask." She tucked some stray curls back into the edge of her hood. Once she felt composed enough, she dared to meet his gaze again. "Everyone else will tell my parents."

"Ah. You're runnin', ain't ya?" A sly smile curved his lips and he nodded. "Good. Ya got a point, though. Ain't no one else in this camp that's gonna dare cross a Daugherty. What do you need? I ain't giving you money."

"I've got that." She cleared her throat when his brows rose exponentially. She hadn't expected him to guess, and she'd actually expected him to try to lure her in. Perhaps his attention was little more than kindness. "And I'll pay you for your assistance, of course."

"Didn't ask for money. Just said I ain't giving you none."

"You don't want compensation for your assistance?" Katherine frowned and shook her head. Words failed her at his revelation and she gripped the railing near his hand.

"It'll be worth it just to see the good Mrs. Daugherty's face when she realizes she lost another one." He leaned on the fence and close to her face. "But you gotta be sure. Ain't no turning back once ya run, and it ain't easy to make it being single and all. If you were willin' to be a whore, it'd be different."

"I'm not." She managed to recover her voice for that, and Hammy's step closer to their conversation didn't escape her notice. "I want a respectable job, and I've got money to make it through."

"Respectable jobs and women don't mix so much. Marryin's what most of 'em do." He turned away to lean both elbows on the fence.

"Marrying isn't what I want to do. I won't be a whore either."

"I figured as much when ya said respectable." He didn't argue, or suggest otherwise, surprising her again. "If you're sure, then be back here Monday mornin'. I got someone that can get you outta here."

"Monday." It seemed so soon. Was she certain she wanted to go this way? Doubts began to creep forward now that the door stood open in front of her.

"I figured. If you get yella, ain't no skin off my nose. Just be here if you're goin'."

Katherine could only blink for several minutes, her thoughts raced too fast to catch up with. When his departing back came back into focus she found her voice again. "Wait. That was too easy."

"Ain't nothin' easy about it, Kathy." Cole turned. "I know what someone looks like when they're runnin'. How do ya think I get them fillies in my stable?"

She scrunched her nose when he pointed to the saloon instead of the actual barn. "I'm running, and you're not trying to lasso me in?"

"You're no whore. You got the looks for one, but don't see it on ya. Besides, you're too young." He grinned. "Come back and see me when you're a few years older and we can talk about you joinin' the ranks if ya want."

She pursed her lips, trying to change the subject rather than let her flustered stammering take over the conversation. "So you already planned my escape without me saying anything?"

"I got more plans than ya know. This just happened to fall in with other plans I got. What else ya want?"

"Where would I go?" The amount of planning she hadn't done hit her square in the gut and she drooped against the fence. "Dominion Falls is all I know. I can't go to family; they'd just send me back to my parents."

Cole groaned and dropped his head back. A few puffs of his breath curled into the cold air before he straightened again. "Just as I thought. You ain't thought this through."

"Well excuse me. I've never run away before. I don't know what I'm doing."

"Ya got brains, right?"

"Fine. I'll figure it out on my own."

"That ain't what I meant. Ya got book learnin' smarts, right?"

"Oh." She nodded weakly. "I've always done well in school. I suppose I could be a school teacher, or…"

Cole chuckled into the lingering silence. "Ya good at math?"

"Top grades in my class."

"Good. If ya don't want to teach brats all day, I might know someone in Chicago. We trade services. She wants 'em respectable for real work. I want 'em the other way."

"How charming."

"She might not be lookin', but I'll ask. Real discreet-like. If that don't work out, I got somewhere else I can send ya for a while, so long as ya never tell where I sent ya."

Curiosity dragged her gaze back to his, but he'd turned away. She wondered what secret he'd want to guard so close, but then again, word was Cole was nothing but secrets. She took a shaky breath. "When will you let me know?"

"Monday morning. Ya think real hard, because once you leave here, it ain't gonna be so easy to go back."

"I'll think. Thank you, Cole." She stepped forward when he started to move. "Why are you really doing this? If not for money, I can't believe it's just to upset my parents."

"Ain't no matter of yours. Take the help or don't. Don't matter none to me."

She pursed her lips shut and didn't bother to try again. This time he disappeared back inside and she turned away from the door.

"You really gonna run, Miss Katherine?" Hammy walked up and offered his arm. "Don't seem right. Dominion Falls ain't ever gonna be the same with ya gone."

"Whether I leave by my parent's will or my own, I'll be leaving, Hammy. Mother and Father are going to Denver. I just don't wish to leave on their terms."

"Ya scared?"

"Beyond belief, Hammy. Beyond belief."

* * * *

Katherine crept out of the house quiet as she could. The sun had yet to rise, and even the mines were quiet. Down in the town she could only see two lamps lit, one far enough away that she assumed it to be Cole's. The silence was so thick, she worried even her light footsteps would be heard in her parents' room.

She'd spent the weekend fluctuating between regret at leaving her family and disappointing not just her father, but her mother again, and wanting to run far away from the dreaded engagement.

Part of her wondered if there was any chance of escaping the clutches of such a marriage without running. Then her mother's stubbornness would again rear its head and the increase in propriety and continual corrections to Katherine's posture or behavior would reassert how dead-set Lillian Daugherty was to escape the shackles of the crass world of Dominion Falls.

By last night her mind and heart were set. There was no other choice for a young woman of her age. Her parents had control, and if she were married off, the control would become her husband's. That was something she couldn't live with. Not ever.

Katherine crept down behind the Jenkins house where she was hidden from view of their house on the hill. From there she took off at a dead run for town.

She wished she could have allowed for a proper good bye to her father, but she couldn't without raising suspicion. Maybe once she was established she'd find a way to send him a letter, just to let him know she was all right.

When she got to town, she slowed again. She clutched her satchel to her chest and crept past tents and the skeletons of rising buildings. The whole way to the saloon she all but held her breath to try to remain silent. Lucky for her, most everyone was still in bed.

Everyone, that was, except Cole. He'd been the one to tell her to meet him at this ungodly hour of the morning. Now, even from halfway down the street she could see his tall form outside the saloon. He bent and straightened, loading boxes onto a wagon.

A large man stumbled out of the saloon, hiccupping. In the quiet town, his voice echoed loud enough she worried it would wake someone. "Well, what d'ya say, Cole? Are we even?"

Cole chuckled. "Shut your trap, Frank. You'll wake up the whole damn town."

"Sorry," Frank whispered, or rather tried to whisper.

"We're even. Between what I won in that game and you shipping these boxes for me, I'll say we're good." Cole patted the boxes. "Address is in your satchel up front."

Katherine stopped short when Cole glanced over his shoulder right at her. For a moment she didn't move, but then Cole straightened.

"Why don't you go inside and have one more for the road." Cole clapped Frank on the back and pushed him toward the door. Once the man had gone inside, Cole turned toward Katherine. "As you can see, your ride is less than discreet."

"That is my ride?" Katherine rushed forward. "He'll blab to the whole town."

"Nah. Once you're over the mountains you'll be good."

"That won't be until nightfall!" Katherine set her satchel down. "How, exactly is he going to keep quiet until then?"

"Because he ain't gonna know you're with him."

"What?"

"You'll be back here, under the tarp. Ain't gonna be no fun, but it'll get you outta town." Cole leaned on the wagon. "It's your best bet. If you leave now, ain't no one gonna know Frank left town until he don't show up at the saloon."

"They'll know I left." Doubt started to tug at her determination.

"But how? Maybe they'll think you're hiding in town. You done it before. I might even let them think you're hiding in my place. That'll be fun."

Katherine laughed at the idea, her nerves easing. She glanced across the street toward her sisters boarding house. Everything remained dark and quiet, perhaps it was a blessing that her sister slept in the back room.

"So climb in. Before Frank finishes his beer." Cole held the tarp so she could slide into the small opening he'd made for her. "Left ya a basket of food. Don't worry, I'll distract. Ain't no one gonna know until you're long gone."

With gentle care, Katherine set her satchel on the edge of the wagon, then hopped up onto the lip. She nodded to Cole. "I owe you."

"You'll pay me back one day." Cole offered a wicked grin that set her heart aflutter. "I ain't got no doubt."

Heat rushed to Katherine's cheeks and she ducked her head. "That would imply I'm coming back here some day."

"You will."

"You sure?"

"You bet." He chuckled. "And you'll pay me back."

"How?"

"Don't ya worry about that none."

Movement in the saloon drew Katherine away from Cole's leer. "Oh, he's coming."

"Go on, get in." Cole waved her in, but when she started to crawl, he pushed hard on her rump until she landed on the floor of the wagon with a grunt. He squeezed her inappropriately bare ankle. "Safe travels. See ya in a few years, Kathy."

Katherine didn't even have time to wave before he dropped the tarp in place and closed the wagon gate.

"Goodbye," she whispered.

# Awakening

**Three Years Later**

Katherine leaned on her hand and sighed. Rather than run the numbers she'd been handed, she stared at the door as if it would make something happen.

"Psst." Melanie nudged Katherine in the side. "There he is again. Like clockwork."

Katherine straightened in her seat as the gentleman Melanie pointed at removed his hat and scanned the bay of windows. The particular bank Katherine worked in employed all women to handle the everyday transactions, while the men handled the larger business of the bank.

All rumor indicated that Mr. Patrick Warner came to this bank religiously for that reason alone. Rumor also said he'd wooed, corrupted, and then broke the heart of every woman that dared to catch his eye.

Katherine didn't pull her gaze away when he glanced her direction, as she had for the past two weeks. "Perhaps he'll visit my window today. I heard tell he's left Marjorie bereft, so he'll be looking for a new woman."

"Katherine Marie, you can't be serious." Melanie gasped and set about rearranging the stamps on her desk. "He's broken the heart of every woman he's approached."

"That's because they were hoping for love and marriage. To be taken away from this horrible life as a worker. I have no designs for the life of a wife." Granted, Katherine had yet to achieve the freedom she'd left Dominion Falls to find three years ago. While Cole's guidance had taken her to a home and a steady job, for which she was grateful, she'd yet to find the freedom she'd sought. She'd never been left wanting for food or shelter, but she wanted more. Travel, excitement, and maybe even men.

Just a month ago she'd turned eighteen and, as per her agreement with the woman that had taken her in, Katherine had needed to find a job of her own and living arrangements. She'd managed to find room in a woman's boarding house and the job at the bank. All of which she'd done under the name she'd assumed when she'd first moved to Chicago, Katherine Wells.

Still, she was doing everything she was supposed to, as she was supposed to. With her coming of age, she wanted more, more than a new name and a decent job. Before she turned spinster, she was curious as to what lay beyond propriety, and she hungered for life beyond her job and the city of Chicago. If she had to start anywhere, why not with learning about sex with a man skilled enough to corrupt numerous proper young ladies as Mr. Warner had?

"Katherine." Melanie set her hand on Katherine's arm. "He's a rake."

"I know full well what he is." Kat smiled at the man whose eye she planned to catch, as he spoke with one of the men in the lobby. "Perhaps if he knows what I'm after, we can come to an agreement. After all, the only thing I wish is what he's rumored to be quite skilled at."

Deep red hues flooded Melanie's features, and she shook her head. "It isn't decent."

"I've been decent for too long." Katherine had kept her head down and done what she should out of fear her parents would locate her and drag her home if she drew too much attention. At eighteen, the fear was subsiding and the burning need for more that had first flamed to light in Dominion Falls now burned bright again.

Before Melanie could protest further, Patrick approached Katherine's window. His smile broadened with every step closer he took.

Katherine brushed an unruly curl back into place and returned his smile. "Good afternoon, Mr. Warner."

"Good afternoon. I'm afraid you have me at a disadvantage. You know my name, and I don't know yours." He slid his transaction across the desk.

"I'm Katherine." She didn't bother with a last name, though it would be the proper thing to do. "And it wasn't a disadvantage. I believe you enjoy allowing your reputation to precede you, Mr. Warner."

"I believe you're right, Kat."

She smiled at the nickname no one had dared to call her before. Once his transaction was complete, she quirked at brow at his continued presence at her window. "Was there anything else, Mr. Warner?"

"You're new here."

"I've been employed here for three weeks. Long enough."

"Long enough for what?"

Katherine shrugged. "To have learned some things."

"Perhaps we could discuss those things outside of the bank?" He leaned on the counter and flashed a charming smile. "Over supper?"

"No, supper won't do." She grinned when he straightened in surprise. "I wouldn't mind a walk. I have a proposition for you, and it is best discussed discreetly."

His surprise melted into a wicked grin. "I'm intrigued. For that alone, I'll take you up on the offer. When shall we have this stroll?"

"Are you free this evening?"

"I can be for one so bold."

"Then at five, right outside."

"I look forward to it, Kat."

"Me too, Mr. Warner."

* * * *

At the end of the day Melanie gathered her things and left without a word to Katherine. Unsure whether to feel insulted or pity the girl, Katherine shrugged and draped her shawl over her shoulders.

Out of the corner of her eye, her supervisor, and new friend Delphine, waved Katherine over. Even though she knew Patrick could be waiting on her, Katherine obliged. Delphine's own words rang in Katherine's ears. *It's best to leave them waiting.*

Katherine smiled as she approached Delphine's desk. "Everything all right?"

"Of course it is. You were perfectly balanced as always. You should try investing, build up that secret little nest egg you've got." Delphine rose and grabbed her own shawl. When she spoke again, her tone remained low. "What happened with Mr. Warner? Did you get his attention as you'd hoped?"

"You mean as we'd hoped?" Katherine could attribute her bold decisions to Delphine's urging. "Yes. And he called me Kat."

"Kat. I like that." Delphine laced her arm through Katherine's and headed toward the door. "It suits you well."

"Not yet." Katherine took a deep breath as they left the building. She was both excited and afraid for the step she was taking. For years she'd known she didn't wish to ever get married. Meeting Delphine weeks ago had firmed the belief.

Delphine herself was married, had been for years. The reason she worked was three-fold. One, because she wanted to work. Two, it gave her another excuse beyond the standard 'Ladie's Auxiliary' to be out of the house when she meant to sneak away to suffrage meetings. Third, her family needed the income since her husband drank and whored away his own money.

Katherine's bond with Delphine had been instantaneous, for reasons beyond Katherine's understanding. In the past few weeks, Katherine had gone to her first suffrage meeting, and learned much about the marriage bed she hadn't known.

Out of all the complaints Delphine had about her husband, she had none about the lover she kept on the side. Her whispered tales of rendezvous had piqued Katherine's interest enough to consider the prospect ahead of her.

Delphine held Katherine near the back door of the bank. "So you are meeting with Mr. Warner, then?"

"Right now, in fact. He offered supper; I turned him down but suggested a walk." Katherine nudged another stray curl back from her forehead. "I thought supper was too suggestive of wanting a relationship. I want nothing of the sort. Although, I do believe Melanie might not ever speak to me again since I have aspirations of bedding him."

"Never you mind that little priss. She's digging for a husband, and she's jealous that Warner looked your way. She's been here well over a year and he's never cast her a second glance." Delphine adjusted Katheirne's shawl. "I'll move you away from her tomorrow. Closer to my desk is suitable. I spoke to Mr. King today about your skill. He agreed with me that though you've only been here a month, you can move up the ranks."

"Thank you, Delphine." Katherine squeezed her hands. "Now I should go. While you said it's good to make them wait, perhaps it's not good to make him wait too long."

"True enough. Go on then. I have an appointment of my own to keep." Delphine winked before she darted down the alley.

Katherine chuckled as she followed her friend toward the street. Even after Delphine disappeared from view, Katherine didn't pick up her pace. Before she reached the end of the alley, Mr. Warner stepped into view.

He leaned against the wall, one hand on his cane. Elegance and confidence lingered about him like an intoxicating perfume. As it often had when confronted with the more refined suitors she met in Chicago, her mind drifted back to Dominion Falls and a brash, cocky rake of a man that had helped her escape her arranged marriage.

His final assurance that she'd find a way to pay him back one day still crossed her mind at least three times a week. When she smiled at the memory, Mr. Warner rewarded her with a smooth smile of his own.

Katherine bowed her head in greeting. "I apologize for keeping you waiting, Mr. Warner. Mrs. Finney wanted to go over my numbers before I left."

"No apologies required. It is only my curiosity that has made me impatient."

"Curiosity?" She tried to feign innocence, even as he confirmed he'd had the reaction she'd hoped for. "Whatever has made you curious?"

"You. Few women turn down supper at a fine restaurant in town. Certainly none in favor of an unescorted walk."

"Especially with how your reputation precedes you, correct?" She skirted around him to the sidewalk and didn't wait for his arm to begin walking. "After all, what woman wouldn't want to be the one to capture and tame the intractable rake, Patrick Warner? That would certainly be a feather in ones cap if one cared about such things."

"And you don't?" He caught up to her in a few quick steps. "Sounds much like a trick a child would play. To act contrary to how one desires to get precisely what they desire."

"I assure you, Mr. Warner, if I cared one nit about marriage I would be married, not working in a bank in this city."

"Again."

"We could go back and forth, but that would get boring, wouldn't it?" Besides, nerves were getting the better of her. While she'd considered the idea he might not believe her, she'd rather hoped it wouldn't happen. Her ability to argue seemed to only rise in short bursts or when she was truly sure of herself.

"True." His cane clicked on the walkway with every other step they took. Somehow they'd begun to move in sync, his hand came to rest on her elbow.

"Why don't you hear me out? You can decide from there if you wish to believe me and take the risk."

"I'd be willing to listen."

"Good." She stopped to hail a nearby cab. When Mr. Warner tried to pay, she brushed him aside and paid the driver after telling him to take them to Lincoln Park. She settled into her seat, and waited for him to follow suit.

Once he did, the cab took off and silence fell between them. Katherine wasn't sure why he stared her down so intently; whether to determine if she was legitimate, or to make her uneasy, but she chose to ignore him.

Neither of them spoke until they arrived at the park and Patrick hopped out of the carriage. He turned to help her down and offered a cheeky smile along with his hand. "You've already won points by not being one to gab my ear off."

"Or did I lose them by not fawning and flattering you with false platitudes?"

"I failed to think of it that way. Perhaps I should realign my thoughts on the matter. What do you think?"

"I think you should wait until you've heard my proposition as you said you would." If nothing else, the teasing word play set her more at ease. Being clever and witty with the opposite sex is something she'd learned in the past few years. While her first job had been as a teacher, after that each job required interactions with men.

Miss Stapleton had trained all her girls on etiquette and conversation. Katherine knew many of the girls were eventually groomed into high class whores, but no soiled dove ever flew from Miss Stapleton's nest until she was eighteen. Those that failed, or didn't wish for even high class work servicing men, were left to learn more practical job skills. Though Miss Stapleton never asked Katherine her wishes, she'd never been approached. Katherine wondered if Cole had anything to do about that.

If so, she owed him more than just her escape. Katherine sighed aloud, shaking her head to clear the thoughts. Once again, a part of her life was in the past, but this one had given her some skills she could use.

"Everything all right?"

"Yes. I'm sorry. I got lost in thought." This time Katherine took his proffered arm and fell into step beside him. "Now, my proposition."

"I wait with breathless anticipation."

"You reputation says many things about you, Mr. Warner. It says you have no desire to marry any time soon."

"I haven't yet met a woman to convince me otherwise," he admitted.

"It also says that you are quite skilled not only at the wooing, but at what occurs in the privacy of bedrooms. Or, as I've heard, not always bedrooms."

"You listen to far more racy talk than most of the women in your position." He slowed his steps and cocked a brow. "You're not even blushing, Kat."

"I grew up in a mining town, Mr. Warner. I've heard and seen things I likely shouldn't have long before I came to Chicago." Katherine smiled, once again reminding herself of why she knew she could do this. "However, despite all the things I have learned, heard, and seen in my life—knowing and doing are not the same."

"Knowing and doing, what?"

"Copulation, Mr. Warner. I wish to learn."

Warner's mouth opened and closed, his dark eyes searching her features. He shook his head and stepped closer. "I beg your pardon?"

"You heard me."

"I did. I doubt my own ears, but I heard it."

Katherine moved to a nearby bench and sat, patting the spot beside her. There were several minutes of silence as she waited for him to heed her beckoning and sit. Once he did, she turned her attention to the people wandering through the park. "I also have no desire for marriage. I haven't ever felt a strong desire to be married to anyone. I don't imagine that changing anytime soon."

"I understand that."

"I'm certain you do." Katherine folded her hands in her lap. "However, I'm not an innocent young woman that prefers to remain obtuse to the workings of the world. I've heard tell that coupling can be either enjoyable or dreadful. I prefer to learn a way to enjoy the pleasures of the flesh, and figure there is no better way to do so than with one who is rumored to be rather skilled."

"Flattery?"

"Fact. I have other recourses to take, but this was my first choice." Well, her first choice over uprooting her current life and returning to Dominion Falls. The rumors would certainly fly then. Especially since she would only return to spend some time with Cole before she left again. She could imagine her mother's face were that to happen.

"What would be in it for me?"

"You get what you want, without a woman crying her eyes out when you tire of her and are ready to move on. In fact, you might woo your next unwitting victim as you lie with me. I have no aspirations for a marriage, or a true courting."

"I still do not believe my ears."

"When you do, I do hope you'll let me know your answer." She rose before he could protest or question her further. "You do know how to find me."

"I do."

"Then fare thee well, Mr. Warner."

"Kat." He touched her arm, but didn't pull her back toward him.

"Yes?"

"Call me Patrick."

"That will depend on your answer."

\* \* \* \*

Katherine poured tea into both cups before she retained her seat across from Delphine. "And that was that."

"So he hasn't answered yet?" Delphine dropped several spoonfuls of sugar into her tea. "I noticed he failed to come to the bank at his usual time yesterday."

"And as it's now Saturday, it's likely to be Monday before I get any resolution." Expected or not, the delay riled Katherine's nerves something fierce. While she'd enjoyed becoming more forthright and bold during her time away from Dominion Falls, this was the boldest move she'd made yet. Maybe it had been a mistake.

"Don't look so worried. He'll say yes. I'd bet he's still in shock that he was the one being propositioned as opposed to the other way around. Men are delicate creatures, they don't know how to handle such turmoil."

Katherine chuckled, and relaxed again. "I admit to being a bit out of sorts by the whole thing myself. I've never been quite so bold."

"It's about time you were. It's about time we all were. Women should be allowed to leave their husband's at the asylum, just as men are allowed to do to us."

"I told you I'd come to the next meeting. You don't have to lecture me today." Katherine had agreed to attend another suffrage meeting, not that it had taken much convincing. The Women's Temperance League was a tougher sell because of their rather extreme measures in some cases. "Or is there a reason for your enthusiastic pining's today, Delphie?"

"No reason beyond the usual."

"Delphie."

"Just a rough night is all." Delphie waved off further questioning. "Never you mind. It'll pass, it always does."

"Until the next time he gets drunk, which is right about every forty eight hours. I know drunks; I grew up around them. Three saloons kept them well nourished."

"I didn't come here to discuss me. So hush."

"Yes, ma'am." Katherine knew better than to push further. When it came to the debate on what to do about her husband, Delphie was more stubborn than usual. Katherine tended to believe it was because Delphie was scared.

Rightly so, as it wouldn't be easy for her to get a divorce, and who knew what vengeful act Harry would impart if she tried. As it stood, Katherine feared for her friend based on what she'd heard of her husband's drunken rages.

Katherine might have only known Delphine for a month now, but already she knew enough to worry.

"Stop looking at me like that," Delphine chided. "We have the whole afternoon and evening to ourselves. Harry went to the casino with all of his savings. Fortunately he went to Jennings' where I cut a deal with them. Once he's lost so much they throw a whore on him. We have time to chat."

"Good. You know, I was pondering a shopping trip today. I thought a new dress was in order, and then I'd planned to stop by the confectionary. Won't you join me?"

"Will you let me be honest in my assessment of all the dresses you take note of?"

"I'd be disappointed if you didn't."

"Then I'll join you."

"Ice cream is on me."

Delphine hesitated, but nodded. "Agreed. So long as I get to pick on atrocious frocks and uppity society I shall be happy."

"We'll go to Minnie Rose's shop first. I honestly don't know how she stays in business. I swear she's color blind."

"Oh, but dearie, her styles are all based on what is in London this second!"

Katherine rose and grabbed her reticule. "If that's fashion, I'll wear pants."

"You could, you know." Delphine winked as they stepped outside. "Sadie and Claudette would be thrilled to have another join their pantaloons ranks in the society."

"I'd never thought to switch, but I must admit they do look comfortable."

"I don't know what I'd go so far as pantaloons, but I did stop wearing my corset. At least I tried. My back hurt when I stopped wearing it. I had to put it back on, although I wear it looser than I did."

"I didn't start wearing one until I was fourteen. My mother forced me to. I've always hated the infernal contraption." Katherine grinned and nodded. "I should try taking it off. I haven't worn it as long as you, and I've always kept it loose. I wonder if I should."

"Next you'll be wearing pantaloons. Just you wait and see."

Katherine joined Delphine's laughter as they continued down the street. They continued on in happy conversation, commenting here and there on those they passed in the street. All the way to Minnie Rose's shop, they remained in high spirits.

Just before they reached the door, the familiar voice of Patrick Warner stopped them dead. "Ladies."

Katherine glanced at Delphine out of the corner of her eye, and noticed her friend was doing the same. They both grinned and turned, but Katherine was the one to speak. "Mr. Warner. Your presence was missed yesterday by several young fillies. You disappointed them by denying them their daily ogle."

"I shall have to make amends by appearing twice on Monday." He tipped his hat. "It is good to see you both in good health this afternoon. Although, I must say I'm surprised to see you heading to Minnie Rose's. I'd thought you had better taste."

"Perhaps that is why we are going in there." Katherine smiled. "After all, a woman with good taste should also know what to avoid."

"Speaking of which. I do hope you'll beg my pardon, Mr. Warner. I see a dress I must simply try for sheer horror." Delphine smirked. "Keep an eye on the window, I'll let you see the high fashion I choose."

"No begging necessary. I look forward to this." Mr. Warner chuckled and offered a half bow as Delphine turned to go inside.

Katherine shook her head. "I have a feeling this is going to be interesting. I've no doubt she'll chose the most horrific dress in the shop."

"That is what is fun, isn't it?" He turned his attention back to Katherine. "I do hope you don't think I was avoiding you, my fair Kat."

"Weren't you?"

He quirked a brow, and gave a small shrug. "If I was, it was only part of the reason for my absence."

"I appreciate the candor, but I didn't need your excuses. My only concern is that I embarrassed myself."

"Never be embarrassed by being who you are. I took notice of you right away; I sense there's more than the proper woman you've displayed at the bank. You confirmed it by admitting you grew up in a mining town."

"I was a child. Children are allowed a certain amount of freedom in their behavior that adulthood is sadly lacking."

"Too true." He smiled and stepped closer. "I have been considering your proposition."

"As I'd hoped you would." Unwarranted heat rose to her cheeks when he stepped closer. She clasped her hands behind her back to keep them steady.

"I am intrigued."

"Good. Just how intrigued are you?"

"Quite. What sort of time do you feel you need?"

"I wouldn't know." When she tried to duck her gaze away, he hooked a finger under her chin and drew her back to face him. "As long as I require, I suppose."

"Don't become shy on me now. You were bold enough to make this request. Remain bold enough to keep it."

"I guess I'll have to learn to do so."

"I don't think that will take you long at all." His lips cocked in a crooked grin. "I have a feeling our only regret will be that you learn quicker than we'd like."

"But that won't stop us from ending our sessions. I'm certain you'll have no lack of new women to corrupt."

"Quite. They need to be wooed, though. You came to me. It's a unique challenge, one I certainly will not turn down."

"When shall we begin?"

"Now is good." He leaned toward her, his lips close to hers. "If you'd like."

"I believe I would, Patrick." Before their lips could connect, a thump sounded on the glass beside them and they both jumped. Katherine burst into laughter at the atrociously colorful dress Delphine wore.

Every color of the rainbow was represented, and there were stripes and plaids in different panels of the bodice. Ribbons wove through the overskirt, and through the piles of lace that created the underskirt. Delphine was making a show of the dress, spinning and posing so they might see every angle.

Patrick held onto his decorum for almost a full minute, but soon enough his shoulders shook, and then his laughter unleashed. "I don't think interesting covers it."

"How on earth does Minnie come up with these dresses?"

"I don't know, but I pray she never goes out of business."

Katherine set her hand on her stomach, now sore from all the laughter. "Well why on earth not?"

"Because, the parties I attend would be terribly boring without one Minnie Rose dress to add amusement."

"I would imagine so. I always found society parties boring myself."

When Delphine disappeared from the window, Patrick turned back to Katherine. "I'm afraid your friend interrupted our talk."

"And I did promise I would spend the afternoon with her." There was a hint of regret she'd not be able to enjoy an afternoon with Patrick. After all, if she had time to think before the event, she might chicken out.

"We can't have you breaking promises."

"How about tonight?" Katherine bit her lip at the nervous squeak that accompanied her words. "If you haven't any plans, of course."

"I haven't. I'll send a carriage for you. The Crumbly Boarding House for Women, yes?"

"How did you know?"

He only smiled. "I'll send a carriage at seven."

She automatically curtsied in response to his bow. "I'll look forward to it."

"Kat." He tipped his hat and moved closer, like he would step around her. Instead he paused at her side, one finger trailing down her arm. "Don't be worried. My reputation is no lie."

Goosebumps rose under his touch. She swallowed against her suddenly dry mouth. "Good to know."

Then he was gone, and Katherine let out the breath she hadn't realized she was holding. Excitement and fear clashed together in a mass of butterflies in her belly. She rushed into the shop to tell her friend, and get the reassurance she needed.

* * * *

Katherine fidgeted with the edge of her bodice. The carriage drove her through the darkening streets toward Patrick's home. She had no idea where he lived or what exactly would occur.

Or rather, she had some idea of what would occur. As she'd admitted, she wasn't entirely obtuse and whores and men were not always discreet in their actions or tales. She didn't know how Patrick would handle the situation, though.

Even though she'd chosen Patrick specifically because of the tales Delphine had relayed to her that spoke of his skill and care with innocent women, a glimmer of nervousness lingered.

An air of change settled around her, for she knew many things would change now. If they managed perfect discretion, things would mostly change only for her, but that was enough. Just as when she'd left home to come to Chicago, the fear she felt stimulated her almost as much as it held her back.

The carriage slowed to a stop in front of a simple, but stately stone-front home. The tall windows shimmered with light, but not a soul passed near them. When the carriage door was open for her, Katherine accepted the driver's hand and stepped out.

Rather than give into her own hesitation, she strode up to the door straight away. Before she could even knock, the door opened to reveal a butler very unlike the one her parents had hired years back.

Instead of a stuffy, grumpy older gentleman, this man was young, and smiled warmly. He nodded in a quick bow. "Miss Wells. Please, come in. Mr. Warner is expecting you. May I take your shawl?"

"Yes, thank you." She shed the wrap and offered the butler a smile.

"I'm Loren, if you need anything, please don't hesitate to let me know." Loren gestured to the room on their right. "Mr. Warner is in the parlor."

"Thank you, Loren." Katherine stepped to the doorway, but hesitated there.

In the room, Patrick sat with his back to the door. The corner of a book was visible around the edge of the chair. A glass of liquor sat beside him, a fire crackled in the fireplace in front of him. One the right was a settee under the closest window. To her left sat a piano, dusty from disuse.

"No one has touched it since my sister went and got herself married." Patrick rose from his chair with a warm smile. "You don't happen to play do you?"

"It's been years, but I did have lessons when I was a child." Katherine returned his smile and stepped into the room. "I don't dare play for fear of hurting your ears."

"Too bad. Please, come in. Would you care for a drink?"

"Please. I'm a bit nervous, I must admit."

"Do you like whiskey?"

"I'm not sure. I've had beer and wine and champagne, and even a sip of brandy, but I've never tried whiskey."

"And you call yourself a mining camp child," he tsked as he crossed to his liquor cabinet. While he poured her a glass, he spoke, "I find that whiskey is good for a bracing blow of strength. It's also good if you're just out to get drunk."

"I thought that's what beer was for."

"Beer is to get out of drinking bad water, made with bad water." He handed her the glass. "It's the everyman's drink. So is whiskey, I suppose."

Katherine eyed the glass, unsure if she should go forward. After a sigh, she lifted the glass to her lips and tossed back her head. The liquid burned down her throat, and she coughed as she handed it back. Once the burning sensation passed, a pleasurable shiver passed through her and helped her shake off her nerves.

"Better?"

"Yes, actually. Might I have a little more?" She didn't bother to be embarrassed by his chuckle. On a night like this, liquid courage was required.

"I don't usually explain my methods, but as this is a unique situation, perhaps it would help?"

"I believe it might."

He returned with another full glass for her, and one for himself. After he'd guided her to the settee, he sat beside her. "I've spent the past day considering this intriguing proposal. I'm used to lying with innocent women, but most of them are rather swept up in the romanticism and my charm."

"And your humility," she remarked drily.

"Naturally."

When she managed to lift her gaze again, she joined in his laughter. "You might be charming, but that isn't why I'm here."

"Precisely. So you likely have more nerves than most. Also, I've considered your friendship with Delphine both a help and a hindrance. She has likely told you many things about what it might be like."

"I've heard the first few times can be—uncomfortable."

"Sometimes it can be. I imagine for Delphie with that roughshod of a husband it was no picnic."

"You know Harry? And you have some familiarity with Delphie? Have you and she?" If they had coupled, it was news to Katherine.

"No. Delphie was married when we met and I don't pursue married women. However, she is a good woman, and her husband is another whose reputation speaks for itself." Patrick's nose wrinkled. He drank some of his whiskey quick, like trying to remove a bad taste from his mouth.

Katherine herself drank a long, slow sip from her own glass to cover her surprise. Given all the talk of Patrick, she'd not expected to find such a personable man behind the layers of charm. She dared to think they could be friends, if what they planned to do didn't defeat such a notion.

"As I was saying. All things considered, your nerves are more on edge. Between expectations and fears, I imagine you're rather uneasy."

"Anxious is a better description."

"Tonight, you have no need." He set down his glass and moved closer. "I won't be doing anything like taking your innocence. My first step with you will involve nothing but pleasure."

She let out an embarrassing yelp when he tugged at her skirts and his warm hand settled on her calf. Before it spilled, she set her glass on the table. After a shaky breath, she met his gaze again. "Pleasure."

"Yes." His hand slid up her leg toward her thigh, the tips of his fingers dancing along her skin in a feather light touch. "There are ways to experience pleasure without ever breeching the walls of innocence. For men, and for women."

"I didn't think men cared about such things." Her arms trembled and threatened to give out in their support of her. The simple touch of his fingers on his flesh sent warmth throughout her body, and her breath began to falter.

"Would I have piqued your interest if I was like most men?"

"I suppose not."

He grinned and drew closer, his lips again hovering near hers. Inch by inch his touch drew higher, teasing the bottom edge of her drawers.

"What do I have to do?"

"Just relax."

When his lips pressed to hers in a warm kiss, she did as commanded. Under his gentle touch, the world fell away and she began to learn a new meaning to the word—pleasure.

* * * *

Katherine stretched from the tips of her fingers to the tips of her toes. The luxurious bed cradled her in its comfortable depths. She'd forgotten just how wonderful a bed could feel in the years since she'd left home.

Against her better judgment, she'd stayed the night at Patrick's, and at the moment couldn't think of one reason to regret the action. They'd spent much of the evening wrapped in each other, although he never did take things any further than exploration and, as promised, pleasure.

Her skin still tingled at the memory of his touch, and she wondered at the utter abandon she'd felt when he'd taken her to the heights of pleasure. The euphoria had been enough to hold off her own shyness and embarrassment when he'd guided her in how to do the same for him.

At least now she knew neither Delphine or Patrick were lying when they said there was much pleasure to be had. Perhaps that alone would make the full experience less uncomfortable the first time.

When a knock came at the door, she drew herself to sitting and tugged the sheet to her chin. "Come in."

"Good morning." Patrick stepped into the room. "I thought you might be ready for some breakfast."

"I believe I am. What time is it?"

"Near 10 o'clock."

Katherine gaped, even as Patrick's lips quirked in a grin. "How could it be so late? I shouldn't have been here so long."

"Of course you should have. You were up rather late. Did you have somewhere to be?"

"I…" Katherine shook her head. "I've missed Sunday services, but I suppose otherwise I haven't anywhere to be. It's seems rather lazy and—scandalous to lounge about on a Sunday morning."

"You were trying for scandalous, weren't you?" Patrick leaned against the doorframe. "Are you regretting your decision?"

Memories of the night before flickered through her mind and she shook her head before she could put much thought to the situation. "No. Not at all."

"Good to hear. If you'll get yourself dressed, we'll have breakfast and discuss what happens next."

"That sounds ominous."

"Not at all." He winked. "Just the opposite."

Katherine glanced at her dress where it draped over a nearby chair. She worried her lip between her teeth, and fiddled with the edge of the sheet.

"You do realize you're still in your corset, and I saw far more last night than you'd reveal getting into the dress."

Her cheeks burned and she dropped her face into her hand. "Of course."

"You don't need to be nervous. I'm not going to attack you; I'm too hungry for real food for that right now."

"Reassuring." She slipped out from between the sheets and grabbed her dress. Once she'd stepped into her petticoats, she glanced his direction. The man hadn't stopped watching her one second. "Are you certain you're too hungry?"

"Not anymore." In an instant his wicked grin returned. "What about you? Are you hungry for more?"

Excitement fluttered in her belly. She nodded even as she ducked her head in a hint of sheepishness. "I believe I am."

"I must ask. Now that you've spent the night it occurs to me we didn't discuss how we wish to handle this. You claim to not want more, but shall we continue our interactions as mere acquaintances, or shall we attempt some level of friendship?"

"I'm not certain, actually." She tugged on her bodice, but before she could search for a button hook, he was behind her buttoning it for her.

"It can get messy if there are emotions involved."

"Which is why men turn to whores."

"Quite true. Although only some men are fool enough to fall for their charms." He finished buttoning and set his hands on her shoulders. "Whatever you wish to do."

"I'm rather tempted to remain as mere acquaintances."

"Then that is what we shall remain."

"Unfortunately…"

He brushed aside some of her unruly curls to meet her gaze in the mirror. One brow lifted as his lips pursed. "Yes?"

"I believe we've already crossed a line. I know you have a sister you miss."

"One detail that can be dismissed."

She wondered if it could be. Something about him drew her, not as a possible husband or anything of the sort, but more as a friend. Much like Delphine. Still, he had a point. Friendship might make things messy. She nodded. "Acquaintances, then."

He led her toward the door. "Fair enough. Shall we dine?"

"Perhaps we shouldn't. If we're to remain as we have been, I should probably go fetch food on my own." The moment they stepped from her room, the smell of potatoes and eggs hit her, and without warning her stomach growled. "Oh dear."

He laughed. "Stay. Eat. Acquaintances dine together on occasion. We'll just discuss politics or something else equally unpalatable."

"Perhaps even argue to further cement our personal dissidence?"

"Ah yes, it is as if you've read my thoughts, my fair Kat."

She couldn't stop her smile. "I'm certain we can find something to disagree on. What do you think of the suffrage movement?"

"I'm all for it."

She stopped short, even as he kept walking. "I'm sorry, what?"

"From what I've seen women have their fair share of opinions. They aren't always wrong either. Why do you think I enjoy women so much?"

"For their sex."

"There is that, too." He took her elbow and began to guide her toward the dining room. "I find that most men lack confidence, so they must find it by lording over women. I have no such need."

"But you go and break their hearts. Isn't that doing just what you say?"

"That is something that can hardly be helped. I have never deceived a woman as to what I was. Not once I have a made a false promise or lured an unwilling woman by deceptive means. I'm as honest as you were with me. If she were to never come to my bed, then so be it."

"I'm rather confused, then." Katherine sat in the chair he held out for her.

"I can't help that I enjoy the physical pleasures of a woman. If a woman wants to give herself to me in hopes of obtaining something I've told her I'm unwilling to give her, that is her fault, not mine. I believe nine out of ten of the women I have courted were the ones to leave when they realized that I wouldn't marry them just because we've lain together. Your friend Melanie is among them, you know."

"Melanie?" She set down the silverware she'd just picked up. After Melanie's reaction to Katherine's admittance of wanting to pursue a physical relationship with Patrick, maybe it wasn't such a surprise. "I had no idea."

"I don't court a woman to bed her and leave her cold. I enjoy the courting. I like having company for a show, or a party, a pretty woman on your arm and fair conversation is better than boredom." He scooped some eggs into his mouth and chewed. "I don't wish to be married, but I won't deny myself pleasure either. Much like yourself."

"I didn't realize." She ate several bites of food, closing her eyes as the delicious flavor filled her mouth. "Oh, this is delicious."

"Mary is a marvelous cook. It'll be a loss for me when she marries in a few months and leaves my employ. I have yet to find someone to compare."

She glanced over at him and grinned. "Maybe you should learn to cook yourself."

"Not likely. I'm not even capable of making a pot of tea."

"Then I guess you'd best work fast to find someone."

"I've been trying." He sighed. "Not much luck. You wouldn't know anyone, would you?"

"Actually, I might." Katherine knew that Miss Stapleton had a few women that trained as servants for employment as well. There'd been a girl a few months younger than Katherine herself that was an excellent cook. "I'm not sure if she's employed yet, but I'll make an inquiry for you."

"I'm much obliged."

"Make no mention of it."

Patrick smiled and continued to eat. After a few moments he spoke again. "When do you wish to have your next lesson?"

"I'm not certain. I don't think it would be wise of me to visit when spending the night would be required again. I don't think Miss Cooper is going to take to kindly to a young lady being absent all evening."

"You're paying for the room, you'll do as you wish. Come now, don't disappoint me, Kat. Keep your spunk."

Katherine pondered a moment and set down her silverware. After she'd dabbed at her napkin, she met his gaze. "All right. Tuesday evening."

"Not tomorrow?"

"I have plans tomorrow evening."

"Ah yes. You're meeting with the suffragettes. Delphine goes regularly on Monday's to Sadie's."

"So Tuesday, then?"

"I look forward to it."

\* \* \* \*

For two weeks Katherine went to Patrick's several nights a week. Her weekend evenings and nights were all spent under his roof and his tutelage. It was their third rendezvous before he breeched the walls of her innocence, and once he had she wondered why they'd waited so long.

Already she felt she was earning the nickname he'd granted her. Kat. She understood why Delphine kept a lover, and her friend was enjoying Kat's transformation as well if her frequent requests for more information were any indication.

On a Thursday afternoon, they walked together to a nearby café for lunch. Delphine kept a tight hold of Katherine's arm. "So he didn't agree to your next meeting? Well, why in heavens not? I thought he thoroughly enjoyed your company as you did his."

"I believe he had other plans. I think I heard him mention something about escorting one Miss Elizabeth Darnell to the opera."

"Miss Elizabeth Darnell? She's rather high up the societal ranks. Might he be after marriage after all?"

"No." Katherine sat at a table by her. "Every indication is that he doesn't. He's friendly with his servants, so they keep him company. Women rarely turn him down when he requires company for a night on the town."

"How fortunate for him," Delphine chuckled, but interrupted herself when the waitress walked up. They placed their orders, and once they were alone again, Delphine leaned closer. "So what new lesson did you have last night?"

"I'd call it a review of all our previous lessons." Kat bit her lip to hide her grin. In a weak attempt to cover it further, she sipped her water. "Before we move further."

"Further, hm? How exciting."

Kat smiled into her cup before she took another long drink. These first two weeks had been tame, he'd informed her. Opening her up to pleasure and the pure enjoyment of being with a man. Next he'd help her explore more creative, enticing, and titillating ways to enjoy each other. "I admit I'm curious what he means. It's been wonderful. How can there be more?"

"Oh, sweetie. You're just getting started."

"That's what he says." Kat leaned closer. "I believe he knows I am curious by nature; he's helped me just enough to make me want more."

"Once you get a taste of the good stuff, you always want more."

"Then I fear I'm in trouble."

"Or in for a lot of fun." Delphine settled back in her seat when their food arrived. "So, now that he has returned to flirting with everyone, are you certain you can handle this? No jealousy?"

"None. I'll only be upset if he ends our lessons for an extended period of time. I wouldn't know where to begin to find another like him."

"Very good. I worried once you became involved in this scheme you would lose your heart too. Even with that head on your shoulders, sometimes things get messy."

"I fear I am starting to like him."

"Oh dear."

"As a friend." Kat giggled when Delphine cast a glare her direction. "What?"

"Don't play tricks on me, girlie." Delphie tapped her hand in a mock slap. "That isn't nice. I thought I was going to have to talk you out of love."

"No. However, Patrick has surprised me. He's rather a good man under the roguish behavior. I rather like him. I have a feeling he likes you too. We could all be good friends outside of the intrigue of relationships."

"Is that so?"

"I wouldn't lie to you, Delphie."

"Then we shall see. Maybe it is possible."

"Of course it is." Kat paused her argument when a familiar carriage pulled up outside the café. "Oh."

"Oh? What, Kat?"

"It's Patrick." Kat grinned when the door to the carriage opened, but Patrick didn't emerge. She furrowed her brow. "What is he doing?"

Patrick stuck his hand out far enough to beckon her toward the carriage.

Delphine chuckled. "I guess you're about to find out about what more there could be. In the middle of the day no less."

"He isn't serious?" Even as she protested, Kat rose to her feet.

"Go on, you silly girl. I'll pay for our food, so long as I get details later." Delphine pushed her toward the carriage before she sat again.

Kat only hesitated a moment longer before rushing to the carriage. The moment the door closed, it started moving again and Kat tumbled back right onto Patrick's lap. "Oh!"

"Hello to you, Kat."

She'd not even recovered when his hand found its way under her voluminous skirts. "Patrick. Where are we going?"

"Everywhere."

"What?"

"All over the city. There are no stops on this ride."

"Excuse me?"

He tugged her close when she tried to slip off his lap. "I thought we might enjoy some mid-day pleasure before I dropped you off at work."

"Here?"

"Here."

Common decency tried to form a protest, but it died on her lips at the excited hum that buzzed along her flesh. She smiled and wrapped her arms around his neck. "In a carriage. How exactly will this work?"

"How do you think, my clever kitten?"

She pushed aside his arms so she could move freely. With a little freedom established she was able to sit opposite him. She met his gaze, and pondered. "My petticoats could be an issue."

"Remove them if you must, or we'll work around them."

"I'm very eager to see how you manage that."

"I thought you might be." He tugged her toward him. "Turn around."

Her breath hitched, but she nodded. "Yes, sir."

\* \* \* \*

Once again Kat found herself in the inappropriate lap of luxury. Her best intentions had been to leave before curfew the night before, but Patrick's best intentions had left her way too late to make it home in time.

She wondered how much it had to do with his current attempt at courting. Once again he'd found himself with a rather high and proper society girl, one with possibilities of a large dowry and vast family wealth bestowed on her lucky future husband. However, by all accounts, the lovely Miss Judith Leek was also notoriously prudish.

For her last suitor she had not even allowed a chaste kiss, and so far had denied even Patrick the pleasure of that. When Kat had questioned him to his continuing pursuit of the stodgy young woman, he'd offered his best wicked smirk and replied, "It's the challenge, my dear."

For her part, Kat would have felt quite guilty over her role in Patrick's life as he pursued Miss Leek, except that she knew Judith was allowing several suitors at once. As it stood, when Patrick became serious about any young lady, Kat stepped back and allowed the courtship to evolve.

Somehow over the course of their continuing liaisons, Kat found herself not falling for the man, but instead attracted to him as a friend. He was uncommonly funny and had a secret kindness that Kat appreciated. She'd often told him that if he let the women he courted see that side he'd find one that would wait for him.

To which he'd pointed out that the kindest thing he could do for them was to let them only see the rake. For marriage was not in his future any more than it was in Kat's. In that regard he did have an annoyingly valid point.

Kat could hardly believe that three months had passed since she had first met Patrick with her proposition. After the first two weeks their meetings had been at turns adventurous and she felt every inch a woman in his presence.

In the dim morning light, she turned her head to take in the man that lay beside her. Oh, she could see how so many fell in love with him, for his charms at his most devilish were unequaled.

One of his eyes opened partway, and his rakish grin spread across his features. "Now how did this happen?" As he spoke, he slid his hand across her waist and pulled her close. Before she could answer, his fingers trailed down her belly to tease her core.

She gasped, and bit her lip as she tried to hold the moan at bay. "It's your fault. You're the one that fell asleep in here."

"My fault, hmm? I think it's yours. You were insatiable, and you wore me out."

"I was?" She gripped his wrist and pulled his hand away, with a great deal of regret. Her brief attempt to pin him down turned into a full on tousle. The rolled back and forth until Kat came out on top, which she was pretty sure he let happen. "You were the one that kept me here past curfew when I tried to leave. You were the insatiable one."

"Fine. Your womanly curves and cries and desperate pleas, your dew-soft skin and vibrant hair, your strong and soft body touching mine, wrapped around me, makes me want more. There, it is still your fault."

She snorted. "That was almost poetic. If I didn't know better I'd think you were wooing me, but somehow I doubt as much."

"Maybe I'm just attempting to coerce you into another lesson before you leave for work. You are right there, and I am right here."

"But I must be at work in less than an hour, Mr. Warner." She pressed her hand over his mouth when he began to protest. "And I must wash up so I don't smell like a whorehouse, get dressed, eat, and tame this unruly head of hair. So no, that does not leave plenty of time."

He scrunched his brows together in a disapproving glare.

"Oh, hush. You aren't mad. You're only disappointed you failed to win this time?"

Soon as her hand moved, he spoke, "Who says I've failed?"

She leaped off the bed before he could grab her and snatched her clothes from the floor. Pure luck got her to his personal washroom with the door closed before he'd caught her. Still chuckling, she leaned against the locked door. "I'll only unlock when you swear to behave, sir."

"Then I guess you'll miss work—for I'll never swear."

Despite the threat, Kat knew Patrick would never keep her from her job. Unlike him, she hadn't vast wealth enough for a personal washroom on the second floor of a home. She sighed as she filled the basin with water. Every time she came into the washroom she thought of her parents and how eager to throw around their wealth they'd once been.

She wondered if they still were as eager for the acceptance of high society. Or if they'd ever bothered to look for her, or still did. She sank onto the stool, her mind drifting back to the day she'd left home. Her ideas to send a letter to her father had never come to fruition, and as it often did, her guilt gnawed her belly.

The touch of a hand to her shoulder startled her out of her reverie, and she grasped Patrick's wrist. He squeezed her shoulder, and she noticed he was fully dressed. "You were quiet for so long I became concerned."

Kat frowned. Once she'd released his hand, she turned toward him. "I haven't been in here that long."

"Fifteen minutes." He held out her chemise. "You won't have time to eat at this rate. I'll help you get dressed, on my best behavior, I promise."

She tried to ignore how his brow remained puckered in concern, and instead snatched the chemise away and threw it on. They worked together to set her corset in place, and she re-tied the laces while he dug through her clothes for her petticoats and crinoline. By the time they'd set all her layers in place, she hoped his concern had passed, but it lingered in a tiny wrinkle between his brows.

"As always, you are dashing." He flashed a smile that didn't quite reach his eyes. "Although your hair is more unruly than usual. Why don't I have Loren bring your food up while you try to tame it?"

"Could you?" Kat sank back onto the stool in relief.

"Gladly. You get started, I'll take care of things, and of course you will use my carriage to get to work. I won't have you late, no matter how much I might tease you otherwise. It would do you no good to lose your job."

"Thank you." She turned her attention to her hair, glad for the distraction from his worried gaze. By the time he reappeared with a tray, she had almost managed to pin her hair in place. "I thought you were having Loren bring the tray?"

"I changed my mind." He set the tray down on the vanity. "Care to tell me what's troubling you?"

"Not particularly."

"Are you certain?"

"I…"

He lifted a brow and met her gaze.

"Not particularly."

"You held the expression of one who was missing something. Or perhaps, someone." He'd blocked her view of herself the moment she'd lifted her hands from her hair. Although, she didn't need to see her face to know the heat of a blush lit her cheeks. He didn't mock her in any fashion, only set his hand on hers. "I know because I've felt the same myself."

"Patrick. This isn't remaining acquaintances."

"I believe we gave that up when you, Delphine, and I went to the Madam Levine's Burlesque three weeks ago."

Right though he may be, she didn't dare enter that discussion. Not yet.

"Go on and eat. We'll enjoy lunch together and discuss things then."

Rather than answer, she sipped her tea. "I should be off. I don't have time to eat."

"You do. Eat." He left the washroom with little more than another squeeze to her shoulder.

Kat did as instructed and scarfed down the eggs on her plate. On her way out of the room and downstairs she was still eating bacon. Luckily, she saw no sign of Patrick, but his carriage waited for her outside.

She made it to work with minutes to spare, and dove into work gratefully. For some reason the memories were painfully prevalent, almost as much as they had been when she'd first left home.

There were few things in her current life she was discontented about, but the occasional bouts of melancholy and homesickness were at the top of the list. Maybe she just needed more to do, to occupy her time, and to keep her free from these bouts.

Just when she'd determined to ask Delphie if there was something more to do with the suffrage league, her friend strode into the bank. For a woman never late, Delphie seemed appropriately uncomfortable with her current state.

Kat had never seen her friend so downtrodden. Delphie's head hung, and she slipped into her seat at her desk without even a wave in Kat's direction.

When Delphie finally lifted her head, Kat saw why. Powders didn't completely cover the bruise around Delphine's eye. Kat's stomach churned in disgust for her friend. Without a doubt, she knew just how the bruise had happened.

Katherine stood with papers in her hand and carried them to Delphine's desk. She set down the blank papers and whispered, "Harry?"

Delphine's lips tightened and she sucked them between her teeth. When Kat didn't move, Delphie finally nodded.

"Join Patrick and I for lunch." Kat didn't give her time to protest, only squeezed her friends hand before rushing back to her own desk.

At least now she had something else to focus on.

\* \* \* \*

"Don't think I've forgotten what the original plan was," Patrick muttered in her ear when he held out her chair for her.

Kat had the decency to duck her head in embarrassment she didn't wholly feel. After a moment she nodded. "I know. However, Delphie's matter is more pressing."

Patrick took the seat beside her, his attention effectively turned to the other woman at the table. "Delphine. I'm glad you could join us."

"No you aren't." Though her wit was not as biting as usual, Delphine sat with her back straight, her pride evident. "Though I appreciate the attempt."

Patrick set his hand on hers. "Would it offend you if I asked why you remain?"

"Where would I go?" Delphine sipped her water delicately. "Besides, Harry has never done this before. It's an unprecedented event. I have no reason to believe it's going to occur again. He much prefers gambling and whores to violence."

Kat frowned. "Delphie. I don't like this. What if he does beat you again?"

"He won't." She sighed and leaned closer. "If you must know, he was upset that I'd been hiding money from him so he wouldn't drink it away. He's gone and cleaned out one of my secret accounts, using his status as my husband to do so. I've not got enough in my newest account to leave."

"I could help you." Katherine set her hand on Delphie's. "I would miss you terribly if you left, but sometimes you must. You just must."

"It won't happen again. I'll be more careful." Delphie shook her head, stubborn as ever. "If I leave it will not be under debt to others."

"That is a foolish choice. Men like Harry Finney don't change." Patrick leaned back in his chair. "And when you have offers of assistance from friends such as Kat and I, then you should accept it."

"You as well? You hardly know me, Mr. Warner." Delphine adjusted the napkin on her lap. Pink hues darkened her cheeks and she shook her head. "It would be inappropriate. Besides, I am my own woman, and I make my own choices, and my own way."

"I know enough." Patrick sat back in his chair, his hands folded on the table. "You are a strong and independent woman, who encourages Kat to be the same. You are both women I'm proud to call friends. You are more the type of woman I'd ever entertain marrying than any of the obedient meek women I court."

Kat and Delphine snorted at the same time, and Kat kicked Patrick's shin under the table. "You'd best be careful. Someone might think you were thinking of marriage as a viable option if you continue talk like that."

"You understand my meaning, and that's all that matters. I respect women such as the two of you, and I'd hate for Delphine to lose my respect. I do rather enjoy her company on the occasion I've been in it." Patrick winked at Delphine.

Delphine pursed her lips. "All flattery aside, I will make my own way. Harry will not strike me again; if he does I swear that I will accept your offer of assistance. I promise I will not remain."

"That's the best we can hope for, isn't it?" Kat sighed when Delphine nodded. "You are a stubborn woman."

"So are you," Delphine chuckled. "It's why we like each other."

Patrick leaned forward again, this time his focus returned to Kat. "Your turn."

"No. There's no need," Kat protested. "It was a moment."

"It was twenty minutes." Patrick quirked a brow. At Delphine's obvious confusion, he whispered an aside, "Kat locked herself in my washroom this morning, and when she was gone for twenty minutes I found her melancholy and the pain of loss, missing someone, etched into her features like tears."

"Your eloquent and overly dramatic poetic rendering of my state of mind is inaccurate and embarrassing." Kat tried to focus on the soup in front of her, but Delphine ruined any hope of changing the subject.

"I've seen that look once or twice myself. Plus, she seemed quite adamant about needing to get away sometimes." Delphine leaned her elbow on the table and rested her chin on her hand. Clearly glad to have the focus off her, she wagged her brows. "I've known you for months and don't know your story."

"Thank you for not helping," Kat muttered.

"Even Delphie has been kept in the dark. It must be scandalous, indeed." Patrick grinned. "Gossip is good for the soul."

"It is not. You're simply nosy." Kat pushed her soup around her bowl with her spoon. "Can't we just enjoy the rest of our meal in peace?"

"That wouldn't be any fun." Delphine tapped Kat's arm. "Out with it."

"There isn't much to tell. My parents wanted me to marry up. I was fifteen and quite ferociously opposed." Kat chewed her lip, unsure how much to divulge. "So I, with the help of a…"

"A what?" Patrick leaned in, apparently intrigued by the way Kat became incapable of finishing her sentence. "A friend, an enemy, a lover?"

"I was fifteen, and you know of my innocence!" Kat grew indignant at the triumphant grin on his features. "I just don't know what to call the person that helped me. Not a friend, not an enemy, definitely not a lover. Just someone I knew. I left town, and was taken in by Mrs. Stapleton."

"Did you change your name?" Her own troubles clearly forgotten, Delphine was actually eating her soup, rather than picking at it.

That gave Kat enough courage to continue her story. "Yes. My last one, at least. I didn't wish to be dragged back to face the fate I'd run from. I changed my name, and began teaching, learning a new trade. When I turned eighteen I was turned out on my own, and here I am."

"But you miss them," Patrick said quietly.

"Sometimes." Kat shrugged as she met his gaze. "That's to be expected. That doesn't mean I regret anything."

"Regret and loss are different things." Patrick squeezed her hand. "But pain is pain."

"I think we all know what that's like." Kat held his hand, and reached out to grab Delphine's. When Delphine completed the circle by taking Patrick's hand, Kat smiled. "At least none of us are alone any longer."

\* \* \* \*

A few seats down, Kat heard Melanie whisper, "Like clockwork."

Kat tried not to snort, but had to cough to cover her reaction. For one so ashamed of what she'd done with Patrick,

Melanie sure liked to draw all the new employees attention to him. Maybe she wanted company in the misery of not managing to capture the elusive man into marriage proposal.

Patrick strode right to Kat's window, one brow already perked. He hadn't even made it there when Delphine was at her shoulder. In the two months since they'd formed a solid round-about friendship, more often than not when Patrick arrived, Delphie was close at hand.

He leaned on the counter and spoke low. "I see new faces."

"Pearl and Vivian," Delphie supplied in a hushed tone. "Pearl is the blond, Vivian the brunette."

"I'd set my sights on Pearl." Kat leaned closer. "Vivian wouldn't be worth your time. Word is she has already played the innocent for any number of men looking for a wife. She keeps turning herself out for the right amount of wealth. Took this job to find it."

"Information much appreciated. If you'll excuse me." Patrick tipped his hat and moved right on past Vivian to Pearl's window.

"I'll never get used to that." Delphine gathered Kat's reports together. "You really don't care that you are setting him on a new conquest?"

"He is my friend. If we stop that aspect of our relationship for a short time or a long one, that won't change." Kat shrugged. "Nothing to be jealous of."

"Just making sure you're still in your right mind. I don't want you falling in love with the man out of turn." Delphie nudged her. "Or worse, setting your sights on something like marriage."

"I wouldn't dream of it, Delphie." Kat winked and returned to her work. She had to admit that she was surprised that even now she felt no spark of jealousy that Patrick flirted with Pearl. Then again, that was probably well-suited to her situation.

Kat tuned out the interaction several windows down and went about her business. When Patrick left a short while later, she offered him a parting wave. The rest of the afternoon passed quick enough, and she was on her way home after a parting hug to Delphine.

As she approached the boarding house, her good mood began to fail. For standing outside was Miss Crumbly, and what Kat was convinced was her own trunk and satchel. Her heart rate picked up, and she jogged the final steps to the door. "Miss Crumbly."

"I don't ask much of my boarders, Miss Wells." Crumbly's Irish accent grew thick in her fit of temper. "But I won't have women such as you sullying the good name of my boarding house."

"Sullying? Miss Crumbly!" Katherine stepped closer. "What have I done?"

"The way you come and go at all hours of the night and day. You've taken up with that rake, Patrick Warner. I have heard the gossip and talk of the unseemly ways you're carrying on." She lifted her chin. "I won't have my boarding house associated with such things. I gave you fair warning last week when you returned before church and dared to attend services right after. You should be ashamed."

"I'm not ashamed." Despite her terror at not having a place to live, Kat refused to give Crumbly the pleasure of seeing her tears. If nothing else, she was honest about not being ashamed. "I have no designs to marry, but I also have no wish to be a boring old spinster such as you. I'm proud of my life."

"Then be proud of it elsewhere." Crumbly turned on her heel and slammed the door behind her.

Kat wanted nothing more than to collapse right there, but she knew nosey girls were peeking out of the curtains. So instead she grabbed the handle of her trunk and her satchel, and started down the street.

Once she was far enough away to avoid being seen, she hailed a cab. Without anywhere else to go, she gave them Patrick's address. The red hot heat of embarrassment flamed her cheeks, but she still didn't cry.

The whole ride there, she stayed crouched down in the seat. They city passed in a dimming tableau of normality. When the carriage slowed, she sat up straight as possible, and tried to push aside her embarrassment.

She accepted the driver's help out of the cab and strolled up the walk to the door. Before the driver had caught up to her, she knocked on the door, and forced a smile as the butler opened the door. "Hello, Loren. I know I'm not expected. Might Mr. Warner be home? I'm afraid I have a favor to ask."

"Mr. Warner is out, but has left express word that the Misses Wells and Finney are to be let in at any time." Loren smiled and held open the door. When the driver appeared with her trunk, to Loren's credit, he didn't even raise a brow. "Leave the trunk there, I'll take care of it."

Kat paid the driver, but said nothing else until he was gone, or even after.

"Would you care for tea, Miss Wells?" Loren took her elbow to guide her toward the kitchen. "While you drink, I could have Tillie draw you a bath."

"Oh. That sounds lovely." Kat was more than relieved Patrick had been kind enough to leave word that she and

Delphie were welcome at any time. If nothing else, it eased her nerves some to know she'd been welcomed.

Without another word, Loren had her settled in a chair in the parlor, a steaming cup of tea in her hands. Though he'd disappeared from view, she could hear him giving orders to Tillie and also to Constance, the cook Kat had found for him.

Kat relaxed more, and smiled. While in most proper households the staff were to be unheard, silent, like magical creatures that did their duty with no one in proper society the wiser to their presence; Patrick had a different view. She imagined his loneliness aided in his tendency to treat his staff a mere level below family. He'd once said if he didn't have to pay them, even that level below would be ignored in favor of treating them as equals.

Loren appeared in the doorway again. After a low bow, he gestured to the stairs. "Your supper will be ready after your bath. I've put your things in your usual room."

"Thank you, Loren. That's more than you needed to do. I'm afraid I'm just still in shock." She rose to follow him, and fell into step beside him on the steps. "Miss Crumbly has decided she doesn't care to have a woman of my ilk in her establishment any longer."

"Your ilk? Miss Wells, you are of the highest class of people."

"Ah yes, but I consort with Patrick, and rumors of my deviancy have reached her crotchety old ears."

"Then it would seem that she does not understand kindness and decency are above all." Loren held open the door to the washroom. "If Mr. Warner arrives before you've completed your bath, I will let him know you're here."

"Thank you." Kat waited until the door closed before letting go of the façade. Her legs wobbled and she sank to the floor, the first tear falling. Where would she go now? Crumbly might be a bitter old woman, but she had a reach quite wide when it came to spreading word. No other boarding house would take her. While she certainly could afford to live in a hotel, it would drain her savings faster than she could replenish it.

What was it Patrick had said? 'Regret and loss are different things; but pain is pain'. She had no regrets, but the loss of a stable roof over her head was a heavy blow. While she didn't fear the ruin of her reputation, she did worry about having to move on if she couldn't find suitable lodging.

Only a handful of tears had fallen, so Kat wiped them away. Crumbly still didn't deserve her tears, and Kat would make do. One way or another she'd be fine, just as she had been when she'd left Dominion Falls.

Back then it had been with the simple help of Cole Mitchell. Now she had true friends. Ones that would help her out of whatever trouble she got herself into. One way or another, she had no doubt of that.

Comforted by her own train of thought, she dragged herself to her feet and stripped down for the tub. The warm water soothed away the last trembling doubts, and she closed her eyes with a deep sigh.

First she'd enjoy the soak, then supper, and then perhaps Patrick's company. For now, the soak took her full attention. The scrumptious luxury of a midweek bath for no reason other than to relax, was a pleasure she'd been denied for so long. She wasn't one to turn down such a treat.

The water had begun to cool around her, and she'd started contemplating getting out when the door clicked open. She smiled, not bothering to open her eyes. "Patrick."

"Kat. What an unexpected pleasure it is to find you here, although Loren informs me, it isn't a pleasure call." He tapped her forehead until she opened her eyes. "Crumbly finally got up the nerve to confront you, eh?"

"Just shy of calling me a whore, but said she wouldn't allow a woman such as myself to be associated with her upstanding establishment."

"Took her long enough. We've been at it, how long now?"

"Six months, I believe." She turned and rose. When Patrick held up a towel, she stepped out of the tub and into the enveloping warmth easily. "Unfortunately, my biggest concern now is where I will find lodging next. Crumbly might be an old biddy, but her gossipy tongue reaches far."

"You should stay here."

Kat's fingers went so numb, the towel fell from her fingers before she could finish drying off. "What?"

"I have the room, you have the need. It wouldn't matter what people said, you'd not lose the roof over your head." He leaned against the wall.

"You can't be serious." She scrambled to gather the towel to finish drying off. "It's bad enough we are friends that still enjoy the pleasure of each other, it's too close to crossing a line. If I were to live here—well, it just wouldn't work."

"I think we've established we aren't crossing that line."

Kat pursed her lips and tossed her robe over her shoulders before she dared approach him. "I don't think it's a smart idea."

"You should at least think it over."

She didn't want to admit how tempting his offer was, so she only shrugged. "I don't know. However, I would like to stay here for a few days while I look for a new place."

"I'll have you convinced by morning."

"I don't think so."

"I do."

* * * *

Somehow Kat managed to make it out of the house without giving Patrick an answer. The man had made every convincing argument on every level. Then he'd taken his arguments to the bedroom, and Kat almost lost her resolve.

Still, she'd made it out without an answer, and left a grumpy Patrick behind. Before the day could begin, she pulled aside Delphine and filled her in. Fortunately the morning was busy enough that Delphie didn't have time to pester Kat for any more information.

However, the moment lunchtime arrived, Delphie practically dragged Kat to the closest restaurant and pushed her into the seat. "What are you going to do?"

"I don't know." Kat rubbed her temples. Her own internal debate had raged all night and morning. Delphie's additional questions weren't going to help. "On the one hand, it is a really bad idea. We agreed it wouldn't get messy, and it seems to me that moving into his home is a great way to muck things up."

"But these days you two are friends first, lovers second." Delphie leaned closer. "After all, aren't you the one that said things had slowed down since the friendship became established?"

"Yes. We've not been enjoying the pleasure of each other's company nearly as much, although last night was certainly an enjoyable exception." Kat tapped her spoon on the table top, staring into her mug as the waiter poured her tea. "But that's rather the problem, isn't it? I don't want it to seem like a marriage, for neither of us want such a thing, we never did."

"It's not a marriage. It's an—arrangement."

"An arrangement I'm not so certain I want any more than I want marriage."

"Well you'd best decide quick."

"What? Why?"

"Because—hello, Mr. Warner." Delphine wore a wicked grin. "Won't you join us, sir? We would certainly enjoy the company."

"Of course I will." Patrick kissed Delphie's cheek and sat between her and Kat. He winked at Kat. "Am I to guess by Delphie's grin that you've told her?"

"I told her." Kat tried to ignore the panicked frenzy of her heartbeat, but her hand shook when she went to stir her tea. "Darn you, Patrick. You couldn't allow me to think on it one day?"

"I said I would give you all the time you need." Patrick shrugged. "I just think it's rather silly to ponder. What better arrangement could you come up with?"

"One that wouldn't require me to live under the same roof as my lover. It rather negates half the point of having a lover, don't you think?" Kat glared at Delphie when the woman started laughing. "Would you wish to live with Matthew?"

Delphie sobered instantly. "Heavens, no."

"Then hush." Kat thrust her lip out into what she knew to be an immature pout.

"If it bothers you that much, perhaps we should end your lessons." Patrick set his hand on hers. "You're skilled enough now, and as much as I quite enjoy your company in my bed, the company of your friendship is of utmost importance."

"I was going to suggest the same." Kat released the breath she hadn't realized she'd been holding. "Only I was concerned you wouldn't agree."

"I admit being disappointed that I won't be able to wander down the hall and fulfill a need as I'd imagined all this morning." Patrick grinned when both Delphie and Kat began to chuckle. "I believe I'm capable of controlling such urges, though."

"You are a man. Somehow I think that might be more difficult than you're letting on." Delphie winced, and leaned down. "Ow. You beast, kicking a woman like that."

Patrick laughed. "So sorry. My foot slipped."

Kat shook her head, and returned the favor by kicking Patrick in the shin as well. "Behave, sir."

"I think you can both agree that's no fun." Patrick leaned closer. "So what say thee, my Kat?"

"I say you said you'd wait for my answer." Kat might have been convinced already, but she wasn't about to give Patrick the satisfaction of winning. "So you will wait, at least until I've had the pleasure of your company a few more times."

"A parting coupling. Oh, how fabulous." Delphie giggled, ignorant to the shocked protest of the table behind her when she spoke quite loud.

"Delphie," Kat tried to chide through her amusement. "I didn't say that."

"What are my ladies' plans for this evening?" Patrick changed the subject, though his grin had grown. "There is a new singer at Milty's Burlesque. I hear tell she's French and *très magnifique*."

"Sounds marvelous. Are the Masked Men still part of the show?" Kat enjoyed the act of male acrobats quite a bit, and she knew Delphie did as well. Their feats of strength were quite a feast for their libidos.

"Of course they are, you minx." Patrick shook his head. "What say you, Delphie? Will you be able to join us?"

"I'm not quite sure yet. Usually on work nights Harry is home at least for a few hours. I might be able to get him off to the casino in time to make it for the show." Delphie tapped her finger to her lip, then nodded. "Save a seat, if you can. I'll do my best to make it. I'd like to see the Masked Men again."

"And you women call me a rake."

* * * *

Three weeks into her new living arrangement, Kat wondered why she'd ever balked at the idea. In Patrick's home she had her own washroom, freedom to do as she wished; and Patrick agreed to her terms of hiring her own chambermaid, which still cost her less than the boarding house each month.

The sexual side of their relationship had fallen to the wayside, and while Kat did miss it sometimes, their friendship was ever stronger for the change. In fact, he'd seen to introducing her to a few of his friends so she might choose to soothe her own urges from time to time. As of yet she'd had no urges for any of them, but they served their own purpose for company and laughter when Patrick was off on his own courting adventures.

Kat went so far as to purchase herself a horse, and often went for rides to the lake, or out beyond the city. The more she explored her new-found freedoms, the more she longed for more. She wanted to travel the country, and perhaps one day return to Dominion Falls, if for no other reason than to show Cole what his help had given her.

Maybe even to thank him properly, as he'd once suggested.

For the time being, though, she was content to remain in Chicago with her dear friends, and live her life as enjoyably as she could. Patrick had guessed at her wandering eye on occasion, but didn't push the matter. She had a feeling he didn't care for her to disappear from his life as his sister once had, and she didn't plan to ever quite disappear like Bessie had.

For her, Patrick was family now, as was Delphie. Her life was rather full with them and her own pleasures. There was hardly time to breathe, or feel the loss that had plagued her in quiet moments before.

"Sorry I'm late." Patrick leaped into the carriage, red cheeked and hair poking out from under his cap.

"Oh, Patrick." Kat chuckled. "If you'd bothered to straighten your hair, I might have thought business kept you late."

"Oh, but business did." He wagged his brows and straightened his cravat. "Just not the business you are referring to."

"What horrible wench has tried to ruin my Patrick this time?"

"It was tragic, it truly was. She enticed me with a flash of ankle, and a peek of shoulder. Men weaker than me would have caved sooner. I stood firm long as I could, fair Kat…but alas, I was lost to the tide of male urges not designed to be denied."

"You poor soul. Clearly you had to, elsewise you might have perished."

He draped his arm across his forehead and drooped with dramatic aplomb.

"The tragedy." She clasped her hands to her chest. "How did you escape her clutches? The siren clearly tried to shatter your soul with her wanton ways."

"I put up a right good fight, and almost lost my whole self to the bewitching creature. I don't remember a thing after her come-hither call."

"Will you be able to survive to make it to the burlesque? Then again, perhaps that's not a good idea. Mademoiselle Sabine might be a siren in her own right. You might never make it through another call, especially one so strong to bring you back to the burlesque week after week."

"I shall persevere. For you must see your Masked Men, and I would release this last wisp of soul for the sweet dulcet vocalizations of the eloquent Sabine." He sat up and removed his cap. With several practiced movements, the unruly locks were tamed.

"Much better." She could barely contain her laughter at the pleased flush that lingered on his cheeks. "You still haven't told me who distracted you?"

"Pearl." Rather than look her in the eye, he returned the hat to his head, his gaze out the window.

"Pearl? Truly?" She tilted her head. "You moved fast with her."

"She moved fast with me." An unusual smile lit his features, one unlike she'd seen him wear discussing any other woman he pursued, or vice versa. "I have not yet fully figured her out yet. At first I thought she might be like you were. Curious."

"We all are, some are just more brazen about it."

"She is not from a well-to-do family. Perhaps she just hopes I'll do for her what I have done for you."

Kat shook her head with a frown. "I don't believe she is the sort, Patrick. If you wish, I'll see if I can't ascertain her motives for you."

"I would not want you to feel I was using you."

"Not at all. I don't care to see you hurt or used. I'll make a better acquaintance with her, and see what I can't learn."

"Thank you." He sagged back against the seat, releasing a heavy breath.

"Patrick?" Kat leaned forward to touch his knee. "Do you find you're beginning to care for this one?"

"It has been only three weeks. How can I tell? It normally takes longer to woo, and I have a better idea of whether I could care for them by then. This time, I haven't had a chance to breathe. I gather she is independent, as you and Delphie are."

"Which you are attracted to in a woman; but you question her motives which gives you pause. I see your conundrum."

"Precisely."

"I'll see what I can do. Until then, please tell me you're ready to enjoy tonight. For we're here, and Delphie is waiting for us." Kat placed a kiss on his cheek. "Remember, thou art Patrick Warner, a rake without care."

"I shall be, my fair Kat. As I always am." He grinned and returned her peck on the cheek with one of his own. "Thank you."

"Pshaw." She waved him off and jumped from the carriage. Before he'd disembarked, Kat had rushed into Delphie's waiting hug. "He's distracted by Pearl, so we'll have to distract him from that tonight. Tomorrow we'll learn her motives?"

"Understood," Delphie whispered back. She turned to Patrick and kissed his cheek. "Mr. Warner. So good to see you again this evening."

"And you, as always, Miss Delphie." Patrick bowed, then held out both elbows. "Shall we?"

Kat took one side while Delphie took the other. They strode into the burlesque together, all smiles. For the night they'd laugh and carry on in merriment as they always did at the burlesque. There would be more than the stage show.

For once, Kat hoped that the woman in Patrick's life would remain. She'd never seen him quite so flustered, and she thought he rather needed it. Her only hope was that she'd learn Pearl was just as independent as she was. That no deception or plot had formed.

If deception was afoot, Kat would defend her friend with her whole heart. She didn't want any of her circle hurt. Ever.

\* \* \* \*

"Come now, Kat! We're going to be late," Patrick bellowed up the stairs. "You'll look stunning as always, but we still have to pick up Pearl and Delphie both. If we're late we won't have a place to stand."

"I'm coming." Kat glared at her reflection. The suffocating summer heat meant her hair was refusing to behave in any way, shape or form. Unruly curls spilled out of every attempt to tame it.

Patrick's snort from the door let her know he'd caught her mid-frustration. "What, exactly, is that?" He poked at the pile of misshapen curls like it might bite him.

"Hush." Kat pushed at the mass, and then sighed. "I give up. Go without me."

"Never." He circled her, his mirth giving in to a frown. "Why not leave it down?"

"You can't be serious. If you think this is horrible, leaving it down would be worse."

"Maybe not. Maybe it just wants to be free. Most wild animals do, you know."

"Patrick Milton Warner. You be nice!"

"Sorry." He set his hands on her shoulders. "You stopped wearing a corset two months ago. I know it's not propriety making you wear your hair up."

After months of debate, and one encouraging nudge from Patrick, she had ceased to wear the infernal contraption she despised so much. She hadn't been alone either; Pearl had joined in her bit of rebellion.

Pearl wasn't quite a member of their little group, for she had her own friends, but she was a fairly regular accompaniment to their party. Kat was impressed with how Pearl had managed to keep her distance from Patrick enough to maintain the relationship between them. While Kat knew neither was the marrying kind, they seemed content with each other's company often enough to say they might stick together. Plus, they gave each other enough freedom to find pleasure elsewhere should they care to.

Kat smoothed her hands across her bodice. "Going without a corset is not so obscene, for most people don't notice. Everyone would notice this."

"Try it." Patrick shrugged. "It can't be worse than this."

She flinched when he poked the chaotic mass of hair again. With a begrudging sigh, she reached to tug out the pins. Once she'd freed the curls, they dropped down her back like tumbleweeds across a prairie in a storm.

Amid her protest, Patrick grabbed the brush and smoothed it over her hair. He moved fast, wrenching out knots before she could wince from the pain. When he finished it wasn't at all elegant, but she knew the knots were out. He shrugged. "Best I can do."

"You are such a man." She snatched the brush from his hand and stuck out her tongue at his reflection. With quick strokes, she did her best to tame the unruliest of the curls. Inspiration hit and she grabbed a ribbon from the counter. She wrapped the bright green strip around her hair and pulled the ribbon into a knot, and bow, at her nape.

Patrick nodded his approval. "Lovely as always."

"We'll see if it holds. My hair has never cared much for the moist summers here."

"You can't see mine under this hat. It isn't much better, just shorter."

While they were on the subject of hats, she grabbed one of hers. She set it on her head and tied the ribbon under her chin. "There."

"Now let's go. Pearl and Delphie will be most upset with us if we don't manage to glean good seats to see the races." Patrick snatched her hand and tore down the stairs.

Kat could barely manage a squeak of protest to his handling before they were in the wagon. Breathless, she adjusted her hat again, tucking the ribbon behind her ears. If she wasn't worried about the wind near the lake she'd not bother with the ribbon at all. "Will we be staying for the fireworks?"

"That's the plan. It's glorious to celebrate Independence Day. Especially with the end of the war. Everyone is truly celebrating again, instead of the reserved celebrations of the past few years."

Kat, like everyone else, had breathed a sigh of relief when Lee had surrendered several months before. Unlike everyone else, she knew why Patrick had relaxed, and why he'd never joined.

Despite his airs and accent, Patrick was the Georgia-born son of a slave owner. When the first grumblings of war had come, his father had turned tail and headed north. They'd abandoned a fully running plantation chock-full of slaves and remade themselves in Chicago. The reason Patrick and his sister never spoke is because she'd returned to Georgia, embarrassed by her father, and married a man who had since died in the war.

Patrick had feared his own sister's death for most of the war, but she'd survived according to his sources. His parents, however, hadn't stopped running in Chicago. They'd left for England and left Patrick, who'd refused to go with them.

Of course, Patrick was a smart young man, and though he was only a few years older than Kat, he'd managed to maintain his wealth even during the war. He'd managed to get wealthier, too. She knew he had his hand in several industries, from war materials to land, and she envied his prowess.

"Have you tried again?" She knew he often tried to reach his sister, but more so since Lee's surrender.

"It's of no consequence today." He tapped her knee. "Here we are. I'll get Pearl and we'll go to the celebration."

Kat didn't push further. He was right; tonight was about celebration.

First boat, and then horse races, and the many confectionary delights of the celebration. Then her favorite part: the fireworks.

Tomorrow she'd worry more about Patrick. Tonight they'd be free.

* * * *

The next morning Kat struggled to get out of bed. Somehow she managed, and made it to work right on time. To her disappointment, Delphie didn't quite manage to make it to work. Kat didn't have time to worry, for Delphie's absence meant Kat had to do her job for her.

The day was plenty busy, keeping Kat distracted from worrying about her absent friend. When she left work, Patrick was already waiting with his friend Aaron for her and Pearl. They dined, and returned home for more pleasures.

When she got to work the next morning, Kat fully expected to find Delphie waiting to tell the story of her absence. However, she wasn't there again.

Kat did her best to focus on work, but she couldn't concentrate. Halfway through the morning, she grabbed her things and left without a word. She'd likely lose her job, but concern gnawed her belly too strong for her to care.

She rushed to the telegraph office and sent a wire to Patrick at home. Within minutes she received a response to wait where she was. She paced in front of the office until Patrick showed up in the carriage.

He held open the door long enough for her to get in. The moment it closed, the carriage took off before she'd even sat. Concern creased Patrick's brow. "She wasn't at work today either?"

"No. It's just not like her, Patrick." She tapped her fingers on her knee, silently willing the carriage to go faster. "You know she even showed up after he hit her. The powders did nothing to hide it, but she was at work anyway."

"I know. I agree. Delphie wouldn't miss work two days in a row."

"I understood yesterday. I didn't wish to be there, either. We celebrated too long into the night, but now that I think about it, that wasn't like her either. I've seen her come to work still groggy from our revelries the night before."

"She's fine."

She didn't know whom he was trying to convince, but she didn't protest. His words had to hold true. Kat didn't know what she'd do if they weren't.

The carriage came to a stop and they both darted for the door. Kat let him open the door, but burst through ahead of him. She raced to Delphie's door and pounded on it with the flat of her hand. "Delphie? Delphie, darling, open up! Delphie?"

Patrick circled the house and peered into the windows. "I don't see Harry or Delphie." He kept circling around out of sight.

"Delphie!" Kat's voice squeaked and she pounded with her fist. "Please open the door. I'm worried about you."

"Kat!"

Panic seized her heart into a tight knot and stopped her breath. She couldn't move, didn't want to dare see, but she had to. The shatter of glass stirred her from her fear, and she tore around the corner toward the back of the house.

As she rounded the corner, Patrick shoved open the back door. "Delphie!"

Kat stopped short inside the door as the state of the kitchen hit her. The table was upended, silverware scattered across the floor amidst shards of porcelain from the plates Delphie had bought with such pride.

Try as she might, Kat couldn't ignore the blood smeared her and there. She blinked rapidly to try to keep the tears at bay. Patrick had disappeared from view, and her worry that Harry might still be around pushed Kat through the kitchen into the hall.

Patrick stood stock still outside the bedroom.

Kat approached slow, and slipped her hand in his as she drew near.

"Go back." Patrick's voice was a tense rasp.

"No." She drew up beside him despite her quaking soul. The heart she'd been convinced was lodged permanently in her throat dropped like a stone into her stomach. Kat gagged at the onset of fear and pain, her hand spasmed in Patrick's. "No."

Inside, a faint path of blood trailed along the floor to the bed. There lay Delphie, her features bruised and swollen, dress torn half off. Kat was sure she saw more blood on her friends back, but was afraid to approach to be certain.

Patrick moved before Kat could gather herself, and strode to the bed. He knelt down next to Delphie. The moment he set his hand on her shoulder, he drew it back as if he'd been bit. "Delphie?"

Kat scrambled into the room behind him at the declaration and set her own hand on Delphie's back. "She's not dead. Delphie, darling. Please open your eyes."

A quiet moan filtered through the hushed panic of the pair. One of Delphie's fingers twitched, but that was all.

"We must get the doctor, Patrick. Maybe she'll be saved." Kat grasped Delphie's hand against her chest, ignorant of the blood now. The tears she'd held back burned her eyes when he turned a doubtful gaze her way. "Please, please, we must try. We must."

Patrick nodded, and after a kiss to her forehead, left the room.

Kat scanned the room and saw the wash basin still had water in it. "I'll be right back, Delphie. I swear I'm not leaving your side. Just don't die on me. I can't lose you. Patrick can't lose you. We need you, Del."

After she'd swiped at her own tears, Kat rushed over to the bowl and carried it back to the bed. She dropped the sponge in before turning her attention to Delphie. With shaking hands, she peeled back the torn dress until Delphie was free.

As she untied the corset, she noticed the blood centered around one spot in Delphie's back. She ran her finger along the clean tear in the fabric and bit back a sob. "Delphie. I'm sorry, this is probably going to hurt."

Patrick's footsteps echoed back down the hall and he rushed over to set his hand on Kat's. "Hold on. Let's make this a little easier."

Kat wrinkled her brow in confusion when he disappeared again. He disappeared into the sitting room, and she heard him rummaging around before he appeared in the hall with a pair of scissors. She sighed and nodded, holding out her hand when he approached. "That will help, but I'll probably need your help to turn her over once I'm done with her back. Any sign of..."

"No. While I was sending Frederick for the doctor, the neighbor said he thought she'd seen both Mister and Missus Finney leave early yesterday morning. They had trunks, so she assumed they were going on a trip."

"What?" Kat cut the corset ties quickly and peeled aside the corset. "Who could have been with him?"

"Probably one of his whores," Patrick said quietly. He hissed and set his hand near the cut in her back.

Kat wrung out the sponge and started to clean Delphie's back. "Let's not discuss it. Let's talk about what we'll do when Delphie is healed. Where we'll go. Obviously we won't stay here, what new town should we terrorize?"

"Kat," he whispered.

She nudged him sharply with her elbow and shook her head. "I've always wanted to see New York, but I bet women like us are a dime a dozen there. Don't you think so, Delphie?"

With Delphie's back cleaned, they both hesitated. Patrick set his hand near the wound again, and pressed gently. Delphie moaned, and a trickle of blood escaped.

Kat sucked her lips between her teeth and sank next to the bed. "Delphie. Please open your eyes. The doctor will be here soon. You're going to be all right."

Delphie's unbruised eye fluttered half open. A tear slipped to the muslin beneath her head. Her mouth moved, but the words were too quiet. Kat leaned closer to hear Delphie say, "Sorry. I should...have...left..."

"Shhh. None of that talk. You're going to leave this time. Just like you promised." Kat smoothed her hand over Delphie's hair. "I can hear the carriage out front. The doctor is coming. You're going to be all right. You have to be."

The doctor burst into the room full of questions and demands.

There was no time for chatter or hope; all Kat could do now was pray.

* * * *

Patrick sank into the chair beside Kat. While she held Delphine's hand, Patrick placed his own on Delphie's leg. He cleared his throat. "I've let Pearl know, and she's sending word onto the Auxiliary."

Kat knew he meant the suffrage group they met with. With a shaky breath, she nodded. "Good. They should know." There was so much to say, so much to do, but Kat couldn't tear herself from Delphie's side. Without knowing how much longer they had, she was loathed to be anywhere else.

The doctor had done the best he could, she supposed, but it hadn't mattered in the end. In Kat's head, her friend had fought valiantly, and that's why she was so much worse off.

"I just want her to wake up," Kat said. Sorrow heated her eyes and her nose twitched against the burgeoning tears. "For a little while. I want her to remember she was loved. I want that to be what she sees when…"

Patrick wrapped his free arm around her shoulder and kissed her temple. "I sent a wire to Matthew, but he's in St. Louis. I don't know if he'll be back soon enough."

She wiped away her tears again, angry they wouldn't stop flowing. "We'll tell her. She'll wake up. Just once, she has to."

"She will," he whispered.

"Did you hear that, Delphie? We need you to wake up. Please, just for a little while." Unable to keep her voice steady any longer, Kat bowed her head. She covered her tear-filled eyes with her free hand, hiccupping sobs growing louder.

When Patrick pulled her close, she curled into him and let the tears flow. He soothed her quietly, and she cried until she was too tired to shed another tear. Too tired to fight when he lifted carried her to the sitting room sofa, she gave in to the clutching fingers of sleep.

She woke to Pearl shaking her gently. "Kat, wake up. Delphie's eyes are open."

Kat tensed and flew to her feet so fast the whole room spun.

"Easy." Pearl laced her arm around Kat's waist. "I'll help you there, then leave you and Patty to say your goodbyes. The doctor and I are in the kitchen if you need anything."

"The kitchen." Kat swallowed at the embarrassing squeak in her voice.

"You've been napping for hours. Some of the ladies came to clean it up. At least enough for us to use it while we need it." Pearl stopped at the bedroom door. "Go on."

Kat attempted a smile of gratitude, but then slipped into the room without another word. When Patrick waved her over, she flew to the edge of the bed. She both sobbed and laughed when Delphie turned her head. "Oh, Delphie."

"Shhh. Stop that." Tears shimmered in Delphie's eyes. "I haven't the energy for tears."

"I'm just so happy to see you." Kat clasped her friend's hand. "You know how much I love you, right? You and Patrick, you're my family now."

"And you are mine." Delphie's smile was weak, like her voice. "I'm sorry I was so stubborn. This could have…"

"Now it's your turn to stop." Kat's voice caught and she smoothed her free hand over Delphie's forehead. "Just relax. The blame isn't yours, it never was. Remember those that loved you. Patrick, myself, Matthew."

"Tell him," Delphie whispered.

"We will," Patrick interrupted. He took Delphie's other hand, and grabbed Kat's free one. The circle completed, like the first night they'd solidified their friendship, they all grew quiet. Patrick cleared his throat and stretched his neck like his throat held the same solid lump in it Kat's currently possessed.

Kat laughed weakly. "Well, Delphie, I think you'll be the one that manages to make Patrick cry first. What did we bet on for that one again?"

"Supper at Chez Jacque, dessert at Millie's Confections." Delphie's voice was barely a whisper. "I can taste the ice cream."

"And you'll have it. You're free now. Free." Kat squeezed Patrick's hand tight. "Don't you worry about Matthew; we'll make sure he's all right."

"And each other..." Delphie opened her eyes again. "And don't let...me...ruin marriage...for you."

"You haven't." Kat shook her head.

"We were opposed before you," Patrick agreed. "Don't worry. We will always be friends. It won't change."

"Promise," Kat added. "We will never forget you, or each other. Don't fear for us."

"Don't fear for me," Delphie smiled.

"I'm not. I'm just missing you." Kat kissed the back of Delphie's hand. "Now relax. Stop worrying about us. We're going to be fine."

Together the three of them remained, hands clasped as quiet words filtered between them. For as long as she had strength, Delphie kept a part of the conversation. When she grew too tired, she whispered, "I love you," to them both.

They held on as she grew quiet, refusing to let go until Delphie released her last breath. In the moment, they both held their breath.

Kat's sobs drew the others into the room, and Patrick ushered her away from the bed. He drew her into the sitting room where they could have privacy. She welcomed his embrace and tried to return his comfort as they both wept for their loss.

"Nothing will ever be the same," she whispered.

"No. It won't." His voice was muffled, his face buried in her hair. Somehow she knew he was trying to hide his tears. "We will persevere. For Delphie."

"For Delphie."

* * * *

Kat sat on the settee, her chin balanced in her hand as she stared out the window. Outside the world went by as normal, but she felt the world had gone gray. While she and Patrick had both said they'd persevere, it turned out to be harder than she'd imagined.

Patrick, for his part, moped about the house. Except for one hour where he thrived on his anger and stormed about muttering about Pinkerton's, he'd done little but remain quiet and still as Kat herself.

Soon they would leave for the funeral, a simple ceremony planned and paid for by the suffrage league. They'd offered to let Kat plan the whole thing, but she didn't quite feel up to it. The loss dragged her down until she found even getting out of bed a challenge each day.

Patrick cleared his throat in the doorway. "It's time."

She rose and took his outstretched hand. Part of her wondered if her eyes held the same haunted emptiness as Patrick's. With a shaky breath, she laced her arm through his and let him guide her to the carriage.

The ride to the cemetery passed in silence, their hands clasped as if the action would hold back the overwhelming emotions. Once there, members of the suffrage and temperance leagues greeted them. They nodded their way through condolences to the small, simple grave.

Kat knew what was happening, she just felt numb, unable to allow any of the people to see how deeply the loss cut her. When it came time to speak, she was grateful Patrick had told her in advance he'd be the one saying words. She wasn't sure she'd be able to speak without losing her thin hold on control.

As always, Patrick spoke with eloquence and strength, weaving his mourning into an almost poetic tribute. When he was done, he moved right back to her side and set his hand on her shoulder, providing her with strength she sorely needed.

The reverend, a stranger to Kat and likely to Delphine uttered words of kindness and prayer that rang false after Patrick's stirring eulogy. Then, all too soon, a shovel was held out toward her.

Kat kept her hands clasped in front of her, unable to take the instrument that would make this finally real, turn it into more than a horrifying dream.

"Katherine," Patrick whispered. He never used her full name, so she knew he was concerned, but she just couldn't make herself move.

"I can't."

He reached around her and took the shovel, guiding it into her hands. "Together."

Somehow she managed to nod, although that might have just been caused by the tremor that ran through her when her hands closed around the wooden handle. With a shaky breath, she shoved the spade into the dirt, and let Patrick help her lift it to turn it onto the coffin.

The world dimmed and disappeared behind a veil of tears when the dirt hit the pine coffin, resonating as if the box were empty. Only it wasn't empty, as much as she wanted it to be. The sob wrenched from her throat, and she didn't fight Patrick when he folded her into his chest.

She didn't know how long they stood there, or what else was said, all that mattered was her friend was gone. The touch of hand after hand to her arm drew her out of her misery, and she managed to get her tears under control enough to realize everyone was departing. She didn't move from Patrick's hold, but opened her teary eyes to watch the group walking from the gravesite.

After she'd wiped her tears with her kerchief, she sniffled. "How long do you think it will be before they forget?"

"Forget what?" Patrick, for his part, didn't seem too eager to move either. His chin rested on the top of her head, and he held her as tight as he could and still afford her some freedom of movement.

"Delphie."

"Oh, I don't know. They'll remember for a time. They'll speak of her and the tragedy for a while. The Temperance ladies will use her as a banner for a time, but in a couple of years, she will fade."

"They never knew her anyway."

"No. I suppose not."

Kat sighed, the tension of her torment oozing from her shoulders and exhaustion seeped in again. "I only knew her a year."

A stranger's voice made them both jump. "But she loved you."

Patrick spun, his grasp on Kat remaining tight.

Kat relaxed in the same moment Patrick did when they spotted the gentleman behind them. Small, almost meek, the man had strawberry blond hair and a crisp, smart suit. His glasses reflected the thin sunlight, making it impossible to see his eyes.

Instantly, Kat knew who it was, though she'd never met him before. "Matthew."

"Aye." Matthew tipped his head. "I guess I am not as you imagined."

Truth be told, the way Delphie had spoken of him, Kat had imagined on some occasions a large, strapping man. Then again, her husband had been one and also a brute, so it stood to reason that she'd find the opposite attractive. Kat laughed and shook her head. "No. I think you're exactly what I would expect."

"Myself as well. It's good to meet you finally." Patrick held out his hand.

"As 'tis to meet you." A light Scottish lilt dotted his words, and his smile held strong. "Delphine spoke so highly of you both."

"And you. I wish you had stepped up during the service." Kat blinked when the tears threatened to erupt once again. "She would have liked that."

"Ach, no. I was best suited in the background. As I was in her life, should I remain now." The words sounded harsh, but his smile never wavered. "I am not one for grand gestures and public displays, but I wanted to be here to say goodbye, and to meet you."

"I'm glad you did." Patrick's voice was tight, his grasp on Kat's shoulder growing tighter. "I wish we'd met sooner."

"Wish for the future, not for the past." Matthew reached for Kat's hand. When she took it, he smiled. "You knew her best; do not let my absence let you believe otherwise. We were content in our arrangement."

"She loved you," Kat managed to speak over her tears.

"I know." Matthew smiled and brushed the tear from her cheek. "And she loved you both. You were her family."

Kat nodded, but couldn't bring herself to say anything else.

Matthew reached into his coat and withdrew an envelope. "After last year, when Harry hit her and closed her account, Delphine asked if I would allow her an account under my name for the purpose of escape. I said yes without hesitation."

"I remember that." Patrick cleared his throat. "We offered her assistance, which she refused. She was stubborn."

"Yes she was. However, she had to build the account slower so Harry wouldn't know. I believe you know she also did some small work to earn more money, some piecework and tailoring by hand." Matthew moved the envelope through his hands, his head dropping as he took a shaky breath. "She'd almost reached her goal."

"Harry hadn't hit her again," Kat filled in when Matthew fell silent. "She told us she wanted to leave anyway. She was saving for it. August was her goal."

"Two months and two hundred dollars shy." Matthew surreptitiously swiped at his cheek, and neither Kat nor Patrick acknowledged the gesture. He cleared his throat. "She would want you both to have it and do with it as you see fit. I have no need for it."

"You should give it to the league. We haven't the need either." Kat held up her hands when he held the envelope toward her. "It's not right."

"She did not think the suffragists active or organized yet. I believe her words were, it is a 'weekly tea party or quilting circle with some talk of freedom and liberty'." Matthew's smile returned at Kat's choked laughter. "I know you agreed."

"I did." Kat still couldn't bring herself to take the envelope. "I wouldn't know what to do with it."

"But we'll figure it out, if you're certain Delphie wouldn't want you to have it." Patrick held out his hand. "You helped her save it, I would think she meant for you to have it."

"Delphine was aware I had no need for the money. My name only afforded her some security in saving the money." Matthew handed off the envelope to Patrick, nodding when it disappeared into Patrick's coat. "I should take my leave. I'm glad to have met you both, and I am glad Delphine had you."

Kat stepped forward, panicked though she had no idea why. "Are you sure you don't want to join us, for lunch. I mean, I haven't got much of an appetite, but…"

"No, lass. I will not disturb your memories with my own. Don't you worry. I will be all right, as will you. Delphine would not allow otherwise. She did not pick weak friends, not after being arranged into marriage with that buffoon." Matthew tipped his hat and turned. Without another word, he walked from the gravesite, and out of the cemetery.

Kat sagged when he was gone from view. "I guess that's that."

Patrick dropped his hand from her shoulder, but laced his fingers with hers. "Let's go dine at Chez Jacques."

"And have dessert at the confectionary?"

"Just as you promised her."

"After all, she did make you cry." Kat laughed weakly when he did. "Don't worry, I won't tell a soul."

"Neither will I." He kissed the tip of her nose. "Come. She won the bet."

"And I get to partake in the rewards."

"So do I. Only fair since I am the one the suffered for it."

"No. We all did."

\* \* \* \*

After some discussion, Kat and Patrick had decided to set aside the money until they found a purpose for it. In the days since the funeral, they'd eased into life again. Although Kat now had no job, she felt no desire to go searching for one yet. For the time being she would exist on the savings she'd built on since moving to Chicago.

In the mean time she had begun attending more temperance meetings and, while she disagreed with some of their more forceful tendencies, she had seen what too much alcohol could do. Patrick called her a paradox, attending the meetings and protesting drinking, while enjoying an occasional drink of her own.

She was frankly surprised he didn't call her a hypocrite, but that was most likely because he understood. Truly, she didn't want the abolishment of alcohol, she was trying to urge toward true temperance. There were no true causes to join toward that cause, though. Not even the Temperance League, which spoke of it in its title but not its actions.

The worst part about the days since they lost Delphine, was the burning itch to move on, to travel, to just get away from Chicago. The only thing tying her there now was Patrick, and she wasn't sure she could leave him now.

Instead she satisfied herself with regular rides to the lake. She'd begun to wear pantaloons for ease of riding and wading in the water when she arrived. In the few days since she'd begun the fashion, she'd found herself more comfortable than ever. Ever since she'd stopped wearing her corset, the layers of skirts and petticoats had been painfully heavy. With pantaloons, she'd become light as a feather.

The gentle waves lapped her bare toes, drawing her back to the beach. She stared across the water, wondering what lay ahead.

"I thought I would find you here." Patrick's voice cut through her reverie. She turned to find him walking toward her, his boots off and pants rolled up to his knees. His smile was warm, and as he had every time they met or parted since the funeral, he hugged her tight and kissed her forehead. "When you weren't home, I came here first."

"Sorry. I find having the openness of the lake before me eases some of the melancholy." She turned back toward the water once released from the hug. "I have something to tell you."

"And I, you."

"My real name is Daugherty. Katherine Daugherty."

"I know. I've always known." He smiled when she spun his way. "One does not keep Pinkerton's on payroll without putting them to use."

"Oh." Heat flooded her cheeks, and she ducked her head.

"For what it's worth, your father has employed a Pinkerton or two of his own to look for you. I used mine to block him. You will face him on your time, not his."

"That's a mite bit controlling."

"Or protective."

"Or controlling."

"Or controlling," he agreed. "Would you like me to let them find you?"

"No." She frowned. "I just would have preferred the option."

"Fair enough. My apologies. I didn't tell you at first because we weren't as we are now, and then I was embarrassed I hadn't told you sooner." He grimaced. "Sorry."

"It's all right, but I thought it was time you knew. You are like family to me, and I wanted you to know." She fiddled with the edge of her bodice.

Patrick tucked a finger under her chin and drew her gaze up to his. "Fifteen was too young. I have a feeling your father regrets his actions."

"He regretted them before I left."

"Will you go find them?"

"No." Heavens, she was far from ready for that. Although her thoughts often went back to Dominion Falls, she feared returning. Her parents, or sister, might still remain. Of all the things she wanted to do, and felt she had to do, facing them was one she knew she wasn't prepared to do just yet.

"What will you do?"

"I haven't figured that out yet."

"I think you have."

"So have you."

"Perhaps." He sighed and dropped to the sand. With his ankles crossed in front of him, he rested his arms on his knees. "Perhaps I fear for telling you."

"Me too." She joined him on the sand, her head rested against his shoulder. "At the same time?"

He nodded. "On three. One, two three—I'm leaving Chicago."

"I'm leaving," she whispered at the same time. Tears she thought long dry flickered to life again. "Where will you go?"

"I was thinking St. Louis. Further west, but certainly not the frontier."

"You couldn't handle the frontier." Kat laughed when he nudged her from his shoulder. "What? I speak the truth."

"Truth or not, you wound me." He clutched his chest and dropped to the sand. After a moment, he chuckled. "It is the truth. I am not the frontier type."

"Will you bring Pearl?"

"I have considered offering. I doubt she will, she has friends here, and a new start is not always as exciting as it sounds. Plus, I'm not quite sure I like the implications."

"Neither of you wish to be married, but you enjoy each other's company. I don't see the implications."

"What will you do? Will you join me?" There was a small plea in his voice, one part of her wanted to respond to. Patrick had already suffered so much loss in his life; she was loathed to add to it.

"Not right away, but perhaps after a time." She flopped back in the sand beside him. High clouds floated by in wispy shapes, soothing her pained soul. "I wish to travel some, first. I just don't know where."

"You'll join the Temperance League's travels, won't you?"

"It would give me some purpose."

"What purpose?"

"If I can stop them from their violent actions against an establishment just once I'd consider it an accomplishment; and if the people of the town listen to me for it, all the better." She frowned. "Although I doubt one voice will make much of a difference."

"You've got an awful loud voice."

She slugged him in the ribs. "Brute."

"Ow." He chuckled and grabbed her hand. "Promise me you'll visit."

"Every few months I'll make sure to visit. Every time I'm on a train or in a stagecoach, I will write a letter. I won't let you go so easy, Mr. Warner."

"Neither will I. Don't forget, I got some friendly Pinkerton's should you try."

"Pinkerton's are not friendly."

"Not true. They are quite friendly."

"Until it's time to strike."

"True." He turned his gaze on her. "If you ever need anything, I am a telegram away. No matter what it is. Except marriage, of course."

"Of course." She took a shaky breath. "When do you leave?"

"When do you?"

"A month. Will you take my things with you? I won't have a place to keep them."

"Of course. I will always have a room that is yours, my Kat." He kissed her forehead. "You are family."

"We must make the most of this month, then. What shall we do first?"

"How about a swim?"

"You're fully clothed."

"So are you."

"Sounds fun."

# Found

Katherine paced the full length of the train platform in Topeka. Every glance her way was ignored, for by now she was used to stares. Her stomach churned with anxious excitement as the steady pulse of the arriving train grew louder.

She spun on her heel and walked back down the length of the platform. When the train finally appeared from around the bend, she jumped in place and rubbed her hands together in excitement.

While she'd only been in St. Louis a month ago to visit with Patrick, he'd agreed to come to Topeka at her request. Over the past year they'd kept every promise. Regular exchanges of letters and telegrams, as well as her regular visits to St. Louis had kept them close. Although none of that kept her from missing him.

As the train drew to a stop with a loud screech of brakes, Kat tightened her pacing circle. She wrung her hands, trying her best to keep from literally bouncing in place.

Patrick's voice bellowed through the small crowd at the platform, "Kat!"

She squealed and spun around, scanning the crowd on her tiptoes. When she spotted him, she took off at a dead run and leaped into his waiting arms, planting a solid kiss on his cheek. "Patrick!"

With a laugh, he hoisted her in the air before he set her back on her feet. "You just saw me five weeks ago. You haven't missed me that much."

"Pshaw. I missed you plenty." She laced her arm through his as they crossed the platform. "I wish I had better reasons for seeing you so soon."

"What's happening?"

"I tried to lean on the women to assist in this situation, but they won't. I don't understand how they can be so opposed to drinking and yet so unwilling to help a woman escape a situation like this. I can't tolerate their intolerance any longer. I'm at my wits end. I just don't know when and how or—"

"Katherine." Patrick dropped his bag to set both hands on her shoulders. "Breathe and speak slowly. I speak fluent Kat, but you're going too fast even for me."

"Oh, you." She smacked his stomach. "Come with me, I'll explain while we eat."

He offered his arm again, and followed without protest. "So, why are you in Topeka? Seems like a large town to try to influence."

"Oh, one of our older members fell ill down in Brownville. We had to bring her here to the hospital." Kat pulled him into the closest small café and snagged a table. Once he was seated, she scooted closer. "They have been gathered around her every day since we got here. The doctors don't believe she's going to make it, I'm afraid. Cancer of the liver."

"Sorry to hear it."

"It is tragic. I did like the old bird. She was one of the ones that actually listened to me and my arguments." She sighed, but when the waiter arrived, turned on her smile. They both ordered a sandwich and water before turning their attention back to each other.

"Of course, this isn't why you asked me to come." Patrick studied her. "You said something about what Delphie left us?"

"Yes. The first day we were in the hospital, there wasn't much to do but wait since the doctors had to poke and prod Eugenia to find her ailment."

"You were bored and nosy, then?"

"Yes." She grinned, glad he still knew her so well. "So I wandered a while. That's when I found her."

"Her?"

"Her name is Bess. When I first found her, she was unconscious and all alone in her room, quite pregnant and…" She exhaled long and slow, trying to rid herself of the turmoil again. "She'd been beaten."

Patrick's brows knit together and he sat forward. He set his hand on her wrist.

"At first I was too upset, too distracted by my own memories to comprehend. Then a nurse came in. At first she only told me what the husband had said, what the doctors would repeat. I knew she was lying."

"What did the husband say?"

"That she'd run out the door the same time he took off in his wagon and into his path, he had no time to stop." Kat pursed her lips. "When I stayed there all day, and returned the next, the nurse was more willing to whisper gossip."

"Her husband?"

"He's been there once or twice, but mostly ignored her existence. The nurse told me it wasn't the first time she's been in the hospital. She said she'd seen Bess several times and that her husband was a drunkard."

"Did you take her at her word?"

"I believed her, but I waited for Bess to wake up. She did the next day for a few hours. I tried to be there every time she woke up the next few days to let her know she had someone there, someone who didn't scare her. Eventually I got the truth from her, she's terrified for her child, but has nowhere to go. I sent you a wire straight away."

"What would you have me do with her?" Despite the harsh sounding words, his lips twitched in amusement. "Hide her in the stables?"

"Don't be obtuse, you foolish man." Kat chuckled. Their food arrived, so she straightened to pay mind to her rumbling stomach. As she ate she rudely spoke around her food. "I pleaded her case with the League, but they wouldn't rally to help her. They said it was too risky to remove her from under her husband's nose."

"Yet they will destroy a man's livelihood to make their point." Patrick chewed slowly, staring off into the street. "When will she be well enough to travel?"

"The nurse says the doctor is going to release her in three days. I was hoping to sneak her out tomorrow or the day after." Kat fluttered her eyelashes at him. "If you would take her to St. Louis and see she's cared for and finds somewhere to live and work."

"You won't come help me with this task? I thought by your tone you were done with your grand adventure among the women of the league."

"I am, but I convinced them to make their next stop in Colorado."

His head snapped back around to face her. "Oh?"

"Dominion Falls. I told them of the debauchery and numerous saloons and gambling and drinking running rampant. They were salivating for a chance at it."

"Your parents?"

"They aren't there. At least, I don't believe they are. I'm not quite ready."

"It's been five years."

"I know," she whispered. When he set his hand on hers, she turned hers over to grab his tight. "You don't know my mother. She is—intimidating. I'm not ready."

"You're stronger than you realize."

"You're biased, but thank you." She smiled and gave his hand another squeeze before she released it to dive into her food. "The trick will be getting her out of town before the doctors realize she's gone and reach her husband. I will have to get her out with only a little time to spare to get her to your train."

"We'll figure out how to do so. Today I'd like to enjoy the day with you and meet this Bess. Then we'll worry about how to help her and her child. After which, I will do my best to convince you to come straight home once you're done in Dominion Falls."

"No convincing needed. I've enjoyed travelling so much, but I'm ready to rest for a while. Mayhap I'll join the suffrage group there, they're far more active than the group in Chicago ever was. It could be fun stirring up trouble I can get behind."

"Stirring up trouble is an area of expertise for us both."

\* \* \* \*

Kat leaned her head out the window of the stagecoach to get as much fresh air as she could. After a year she should be used to riding in a stagecoach with these women, but this time around her nerves made everything intolerable. Not even the beauty of the snowcapped mountains in the distance eased her distress.

Eugenia had passed the night before the plan to remove Bess from the hospital. In the end, Kat was sure that had worked in her favor, for she didn't have to put on a dress and hat and try to hide from a doctor once Bess was safe.

Patrick had promised to send a telegram to Dominion Falls once he and Bess were safe in St. Louis, and to keep her informed of Bess's progress. Kat was relieved she'd been able to help the woman escape a fate like Delphie's, but couldn't fully enjoy it.

Not with her old hometown looming in the distance. Shockingly, there were buildings everywhere now. As they'd paused on the mountain pass, Kat had been able to get a good look. The settlement north of town was now filled with homes, and the richer homes on the hill had grown from just their old house to several homes.

The town itself now had buildings lining the T-shaped roads. Tents still surrounded the main portion of town, and on their current approach she saw the first sign of carts lining the street.

Anxiety twisted her stomach tighter and she pulled her head back in the carriage. After she'd slid the curtain closed, she fiddled with her handkerchief. She hadn't yet told the women this would be her last stop with them, and she would once again do her best to make sure they didn't take things too far.

"You grew up here?" Lottie, the young woman closest to Kat's own age spoke up. Her nose wrinkled as she peeked out of the curtain. "How…quaint."

"It was better then, not so many buildings." Kat felt frisky enough to rile Lottie. The woman acted so prim and proper, but Kat knew her to be a hypocrite. At least Kat was honest about her dislike of some of what the league did. Lottie just drank and made time with men in every town they went to right behind the other women's back.

"Well, I guess it explains some things." Lottie eyed Kat's pantaloons in disdain.

"Oh, please. I only started wearing these a year ago. Growing up here had little to do with my fashion choice." Kat smirked. "I'm not ashamed of what I am, certainly not of where I came from. I liked growing up here. It was wilder, freer, and dangerous at times."

Lottie's reply was cut off with a sharp jolt of the carriage when the stagecoach stopped suddenly.

Kat didn't wait for Lottie's retort, or the driver. Instead, she reached out of the window and opened the door. She leaped out into the street, not surprised by the constant bustle of activity around her.

Her smile brightened as she turned, taking in the sights, and smells, of the town. The unease and tension slipped away and her shoulders dropped. She was home.

The other women exited the stagecoach once the driver brought about the steps, and began to congregate to discuss where they'd stay.

"Well, Katherine?" Lottie's nasally tone interrupted Kat's enjoyment of the crowded street. "This is your town? Where do we stay?"

"I haven't been here in five years. I haven't the faintest idea. Half of these buildings didn't even exist then." Kat glared at Lottie. "If it's still there, my sister had a boarding house down the street that way across from the saloon. I wouldn't know if there's a proper hotel now or not. Go ask someone."

Lottie harrumphed and spun, leading the ladies to the general store.

Kat shook off her annoyance and began to wonder where she herself would stay. If the ladies chose her sister's boarding house she certainly wouldn't be joining them.

"Just give me that mail bag." A familiar voice called behind her. A gentleman with careworn features, twenty years her senior glared at the driver. Norman Woodward, who had run the telegraph office when she'd lived here, still did if his call for the mail was any indicator. "Took ya long enough to get here. Supply wagon was here three days ago."

"We crossed paths with them coming over the mountain," Kat interjected before the driver could respond. If nothing else, it would be interesting to see if he remembered her. "Our driver was kind enough to help them fix their broken wheel. That's why we're late."

"Well, that's just…" Norman's words trailed off and he studied her. "I know you."

"Are you sure?" Kat grinned and set her hand on her hip. Unsurprisingly, the man scanned her from top to bottom, his nose wrinkling at her pantaloons. "Or did you once and not any longer?"

"Katherine Daugherty. What have you done to yourself?"

"Well, Norman." She chuckled when he grumbled about her using his proper name. "I went off and grew up. That is allowed, isn't it? Also, I go by Kat now. Katherine doesn't suit me so well these days."

"See you're as brash and unseemly as ever."

"Oh no, I'm far worse now."

"Your parents had a right fit when you disappeared. Tore the town up looking for ya." Norman almost smiled. "Funniest damn thing I ever seen when your Ma crawled along looking under porches for you."

"A sight I wish I could have seen myself, but I'm glad I was far away for it." Kat pointed to her trunk for the driver. "Tell me, Norman. Is there a proper hotel these days, or just my sister's place still?"

"There's a hotel, just opened. Called the Silver Saddle. Two doors down from your sister, but they got gambling and whores."

"Sounds perfect. Cole Mitchell never turned his into a hotel, then? Even large as it is? What a pity."

"Nope. His place is best for whoring, though."

"And you would know this how?" Kat laughed when he turned his back on her. "Good seeing you again, Norman."

Kat arranged to have her bags sent to the hotel, then headed there herself to get a room. Rather than rush, she strolled down the street to take in all the new buildings and businesses. A few familiar faces did a double take, but no one spoke up to call out to her. Perhaps they weren't sure it was actually her. Five years was a long time.

The building next to the Silver Saddle stopped her in her tracks as she took in the sign. A combination lawyers office and clinic had to be the most unique thing she'd seen yet in her life. Even more so was the doctor's name: Caroline Pearson.

Kat couldn't keep her surprise to herself. "A woman doctor?"

A familiar, sexy timbre of a voice sent a shiver down her spine. Cole Mitchell himself muttered nearby, "Just got here six months ago. Her husband is pushing as many people as he can into her care."

"Cole Mitchell."

"Kathy Daugherty."

She turned around and smiled. "I go by Kat now."

"Sure thing, Kathy." He leaned against the building's post, all six foot plus of him on display for her enjoyment. The wicked grin he wore let her know he didn't miss her perusal. "Didn't expect you back here so soon."

"Soon? It's been five years. I made sure my parents were well ensconced in Denver before I came." She leaned back against the building as he took his own turn. "I thought I should return home for a while."

"That so? What about them Temperance ladies you got off the coach with?"

"I came with them. It remains to be seen if I leave with them."

"You? With the temperance biddies?"

"In theory I agree with some of their points, not all. Plus, I was able to travel some of this country instead of being tied down to one city." She shrugged. "I might have suggested this camp. What with all the saloons it had when I left."

"Down to three now, mine's still the busiest. And it's a town now."

"Really? My mother's doing?" She knew her mother had wanted to incorporate Dominion Falls since they set up camp. No one had ever managed to organize enough to do as much.

"Nah. Pretty much everyone realized the train wouldn't come unless they worked for it. Made a real government and everything." He chuckled. "Lasted long enough to make the town, then fell apart."

"Well, I should go get a room at the Silver Saddle."

"Ya won't like it there."

"Why on earth would you say such a thing? You don't know me, Cole."

"Just a guess. Swing by the saloon for a drink later." He winked. "If you want. I know you're opposed to drinking and all."

"I'm opposed to excess, not drinking." She pushed off the glass and started toward the hotel. "As for drinking at your saloon, I suppose we'll see."

"Kathy." He hadn't moved when she turned around. Only his gaze had followed her. His sly grin returned. "Bein' away did ya good. Lookin' forward to my reward."

"You're presumptuous as ever."

"And you ain't fifteen no more."

"I'm certainly not." She turned away from his chuckle, not bothering to hide her own grin. Unfortunately, the moment she stepped into the hotel, her grin faded. Loathed as she was to admit it, Cole was right as rain.

To her right were gambling tables littered with a few men and some whores one might call high class. The bar stretched along the wall to her left, with cages along the back wall not unlike the bank windows she used to sit behind.

None of that was what bothered her, though. No, it was the overdone opulence and gilt the owner had thrown on every surface. Maybe he wanted to class the business up in this dirty little town to try to attract future train customers, but it was obscene.

Kat wrinkled her nose and considered turning around to leave, but made herself stand still. Only other place to stay was her sisters. She supposed she could pester Cole for a room, but she wouldn't allow him another excuse to push for repayment—not yet, at least.

A man of moderate height with a styled black moustache approached. His suit was well cut and his cravat was held in place with a bright silver pin. The smarmy grin he wore made Kat itch to slap him before he even spoke. "May I help you?"

"I was hoping to get a room for a few nights." If she decided to stay in town, she'd have to look for another place to stay. Between the extravagance and the man before her, she really didn't want to stay here. "Do you have any available?"

The man looked her over and nodded. "I do. There's a discounted rate for company if you wish it while you're here."

"I don't." She smiled pleasant as she could at the insinuation. While some of the women Patrick had brought home had suggested such a thing, she found herself with no desire toward women. This man's assumption only lowered her already poor regard for him. "Just a room."

"Certainly. I'm Guy Forrester. I'm the owner of this establishment. And you are?"

"Katherine Wells." For the time being she'd use her assumed name. No reason to let this man know who she really was just yet. "I've arranged to have my bags brought here, and if you'll show me my room, I'd like to freshen up after the ride in the stagecoach."

"Certainly. Right this way, Miss Wells."

Kat followed him to the room he offered, and closed the door in his face when he turned to offer her something else. First, she'd clean up, and then she'd get food. After that, the sky was the limit. At least until the ladies managed to corral her again.

For the next few days she'd stay in their good graces and make the requisite rounds to the saloons. At least until she could learn their plans and warn the appropriate saloon owner to prepare for a fight.

Then she would break ties and figure out what to do next. Whether it would be to remain in Dominion Falls or head to St. Louis, she didn't know yet.

The openness of the possibilities ahead of her satisfied her enough.

\* \* \* \*

Kat emerged from the small saloon tent to take a deep breath of fresh air. Inside, her fellow ladies were continuing to pray for the sinners in their loudest voices, but they underestimated how strong the miners in the town drank. Most of the men ignored the women as nothing more than the pesky flies buzzing about them.

"Lookie here." Cole sat atop a large horse, grinning down at her. "Maybe ya do drink after all."

"My group is inside, praying for the sinners." Kat tried, but was unable to keep the derisive tone from her voice. "I decided to get some fresh air."

Cole hopped off his horse and started down the street toward his stables. If he'd expected her to follow, he was right. Only because she was glad for the excuse of an escape. "Can't imagine they'll be doin' much at Tiny's place."

"Ah, but Tiny's is an easy first target. It's much easier to clear a small saloon tent than a larger saloon with whores to boot." Kat kept stride beside him easily, her hands clasped in front of her. "Are you ready for company? I expect them to be at your place tomorrow. I believe they're going to the Silver Saddle this afternoon."

"Savin' me for last?"

"Well, as you pointed out, yours is the busiest saloon in town."

"So you started with this after Chicago, eh?"

She shrugged. "Like I said, it gave me an excuse to leave and travel. I do believe men should practice more temperance, and leave behind such excess enjoyment. However, I don't believe in destroying the existence of alcohol. I enjoy some from time to time myself."

"I thought you might." He opened the gate to the corral and urged his horse to go through. Once it was closed, he turned to face her. "Care for one now?"

"Yes." She didn't hesitate, and even led the way to the front of his saloon. If any of the women questioned, she'd simply say she was talking to him in advance. After all, knowing the owner prior could create an influence they didn't have.

"What d'ya like?"

"I doubt you have brandy, do you?"

"No. My customers prefer beer and whiskey, with an occasional call for gin."

She sighed. "Shame. Fine, I'll have whiskey." Certainly Patrick had taught her the pleasures of whiskey, but she didn't have to reveal all to Cole, he'd sure never do that with anyone else.

For the whole time Cole had been in Dominion Falls, no one ever knew much about him. Where he came from, or who he was. She could vaguely remember that he didn't start out a blatant rake, but it hadn't taken him long to fall into a role that appeared to suit him quite well.

Kat didn't mind. Unlike her experience with Patrick, she'd learned to enjoy men's company without forming friendships. This time would be no different, when and if she allowed it to happen. Then again, with the tingles that climbed up her arm when it brushed with his, maybe she would allow it.

He pushed open the door to the saloon. "Sorry ya gotta settle for whiskey."

"You don't sound in the least bit sorry."

"That's 'cause I ain't."

She laughed and strode with him to the bar, taking a seat next to an older gentleman. "Just pour the whiskey and stop trying to charm me."

"I don't need charm." Cole winked and set two glasses on the bar. "Hammy. Look who came back to Dominion Falls."

When the man turned to face her, Kat almost fell out of her chair. She hadn't recognized Gilbert Hamm at all at first. In the years since she'd left he'd gotten scruffier, if possible, and a goofy half-smile lit his features. "Well, I'll be. Katherine Daugherty."

"You can call me Kat now." She set her hand on his shoulder. "Hammy, I am happy to see you again."

Cole caught her glance, and nodded. "Ya know, you got to thank that fancy lady doc that you're seein' him at all."

"I, what? Why?" Her grip on Hammy's shoulder tightened. "What happened?"

"Doc says I had a stroke." Hammy's words were slightly slurred, and he spoke slow and deliberate. "I right near died."

Cole nodded, his lips thin. "That lady doc saved him. Fixed him up real good. He's still a rotten drunk, though."

Kat laughed because she was supposed to, and because Hammy did, but couldn't put much feeling behind it. "Well then I'll have to thank her."

"Eh. I already did. Got her checkin' on my whores regular. Pretty much the only work that lady gets." Cole poured their whiskey. "Now drink up."

Without argument, Kat picked up her glass and tossed back the whiskey. The familiar burn down her throat, and warm aftershiver washed away her lingering melancholy. "Well, that's good of you then, Cole."

"Naw, it ain't." Cole's wicked grin returned. "I like havin' her around. Bet she's gonna be a fun one in my bed one day."

"What?" Kat scoffed. "You expect a woman doctor to come to your bed? One that's married? How do you propose such a thing would happen?"

"I said you'd repay me one day, and here you are."

"I'm not in your bed."

"Yet."

Kat quirked a brow and leaned her forearms on the bar. "There is no greater way to convince a woman to run far, then to be so sure she will run close."

"You ain't running."

She pursed her lips and tossed back the fresh glass he'd poured her. Once she'd pushed it aside, she stood. "No, but I am walking. Thank you for the drink. How much do I owe you?"

"This one's on me." He winked.

"Adding it to my account?"

"Ya could say that."

She turned her attention to Hammy. "It was good to see you again, Hammy. I hope I'll see you again soon."

"I'll be 'round." Hammy raised his glass before he guzzled it down.

Kat had only just stepped on the porch when her sister tore out of the boarding house. Martha's once rich brown hair had grayed even further making her appear almost older than their own mother.

While Kat had managed to avoid Martha so far, she had no doubt word had gotten around to the woman. In a small town like this, it took no time at all.

Martha stormed across the street toward Kat. "Katherine Marie Daugherty!"

"I go by Kat now, and you aren't my mother, so I won't take whatever scolding you have in mind." Kat met her sister calm as could be. After the past five years, these days her sisters overbearing and uptight personality had little effect. After all, she'd faced worse foes—and she'd spent the past year in the company of equally repressed women. "I wonder what happened to you."

Martha stopped short, her features paled. "I beg your pardon?"

"You were once uninhibited enough to cheat on a wonderful guy with an Indian, not to mention getting pregnant out of wedlock and eloping." Kat sighed and shook her head. "Now you're more repressed than my compatriots. Hard to believe I once thought you to be fun."

"I…Katherine!"

"I told you, it's Kat." She turned her back on her sister and started down the boardwalk, leaving her sister in the muck of the street. Part of her worried Martha would report her presence in town to their parents, but she imagined Martha wanted to see them even less than she did.

* * * *

The leader of the Temperance group, Helen Bertrand, paced back and forth. By now Kat was familiar with the routine.

Helen would get herself keyed up so that she might get the others keyed up to agree to the next step. She'd already loudly denounced Cole's saloon as the worst of the bunch, which would make him a prime target.

At first Kat would argue until she was hoarse, but time had softened her arguments. Often instead, she'd merely protested, and then gone to the saloon Helen chose as prime target and attempt to warn the owner. Unfortunately she wasn't always successful, many of the saloon owners dismissed her as an annoying, histrionic woman.

Because of that, many saloons had been left with hefty damages in the wake of the women in this room. Kat saw no promise in destroying a person's livelihood. For where you destroy one, often two more would spring up in its place.

In the past few months she'd begun to believe with all honesty that Helen enjoyed reaching the point of violence. There was no sign of change now as, true to form, Helen quoted irrelevant scripture once again to boost her cause. "As it says in first Samuel, chapter fifteen, verse eighteen: 'Go and utterly destroy the sinners…and fight against them until they are exterminated'."

Kat bit her tongue to hide her sigh and one of her standard retorts of scripture. No amount of 'judge not' or 'let he who is without sin' ever made a lick of difference. She toyed with the teacup on her saucer for a few minutes before she realized every eye was on her. She frowned and straightened. "Yes?"

"No protest this time?" Lottie's eyes narrowed in suspicion. "That is your standard approach, is it not?"

"As women who are beaten by their husband would tell you, you can only take so much berating before you cave to it. No matter what I say, you'll do as you please." Kat rose to her feet. "And so I'm leaving. I came along in hopes of helping some men learn temperance, not to destroy the livelihood of dozens of men who have no other trade."

"We have changed lives." Helen held her bible close to her chest. "Sometimes it takes a strong hand to enforce such a thing."

"No. What you have done is bullied and pressured. You've interrupted men while in the sauce and tried to speak reason to their drunken minds. Perhaps on purpose because you knew then they wouldn't listen and you'd have an excuse to take up your hatchet." Kat brushed past Helen. "I want no part of such destruction. I never did. This call to arms is not what I signed up for."

"Quiet women don't change the world," Helen objected.

"You don't have to take up a hatchet to be heard," Kat countered. "I am plenty loud without it. Plus, as I am, many men have listened to me. Perhaps I'll be far more effective without the saddle of your infractions weighing my voice down."

Kat turned her back on their gasps and murmurs and strode from the boarding house. Part of her wanted to just go flying across the street to the saloon to warn Cole, but if she did so the women would see and change their plan.

Instead, she turned and walked calmly back to the hotel. Once the world was quiet, she would go to warn Cole. For once, perhaps they might listen. Then maybe she'd feel her debt repaid, and could enjoy her pleasures without feeling like a whore.

Without a word to anyone, she passed through the casino and climbed the stairs to her room. She had the good fortune of a front room with access to the balcony, so she wouldn't have to pass through again on her way out.

Three days she'd stayed at the Silver Saddle, and every day she hated it more. The proprietor was not only over-attentive in his consideration of her well-being; she'd learned in her time staying there he was also business partners with Jackson Krenshaw.

Kat shuddered at the thought of seeing the man that had bought her parents house. From all she'd heard, he was as loathsome as a snake. He was all pseudo-cunning and cruel actions, not to mention his bold display of his wealth.

She managed to slip into her room quick enough to avoid being seen by Guy, and locked the door behind her. In just a few hours when the town was quiet, she'd make her move. In the interim, she'd get her things gathered into her trunk, and then read.

Sometime the next day she hoped to find somewhere else to stay. Cora had been kind enough to offer a small room at the general store and restaurant she ran with her husband Kelly. Kat seriously considered the prospect, since she had few others on the horizon.

Considering she had no idea how long she'd stay, it was premature to search for a permanent residence. For all she knew, she might just pack up and head to St. Louis before the month was out. Once the Temperance group was gone, she wasn't sure just what she'd do with herself.

Packing took longer than expected, and by the time she was done the town had already grown quieter. She gathered her book and sat near the door to keep an eye on the saloon across the way.

Two hours and three chapters later Graham was tossing men out on their drunken rear ends. She frowned, unwilling to cross paths with the man Cole had apparently taken on as a business partner without explanation.

Rumors had swirled about a young whore Cole had taken in for two years before shuffling her off just as quiet as her arrival; especially since at the same time of her arrival he asked Graham to join in running the saloon. Fiercely independent as Cole was, everyone was surprised he'd let in a partner of any kind—business or pleasure.

They'd thought maybe with the new partner he'd turn the saloon into a hotel, or add in a casino, but none of that happened. The saloon remained unchanged, Cole's mood had soured supposedly, though Kat saw little sign of it in their interactions, and now Graham's drunken benders were facilitated by his ownership, and gave him a certain power to use his anger to beat up more men under the guise of order in the saloon.

Kat set her book down and rose, closing the door behind her. Into the quiet of the night, she slipped down the stairs. By the time she reached the boardwalk, Cole was outside bidding farewell to Graham.

She lingered until Graham was well down the street and only the flare up of Cole's cigar when he dragged on it remained. With a careful step she slipped between two vendor carts into the muddy street. One benefit to changing to pantaloons was not having to keep her skirts elevated to avoid the muck of small town roads, and as always she was grateful for that small benefit.

When she landed on the boards across the street, the light of the cigar turned her way. Inwardly she was both grateful they had yet to install street lamps, and upset by it. She'd appreciate seeing his face when she approached, but was glad the dark hid her from any prying eyes.

Either way, by the time she got close, Cole's chuckle reached her ear. When he himself reached for her, she side-stepped him to the porch. "Easy there, Cole. I didn't come for fun, no matter how powerful you think your charms are."

"I don't think—I know."

"I don't think you know, either." Despite his grumbled curse of a response, Kat laughed into the quiet night. "I came to warn you of the ladies' plans."

"That so?"

"If you care to listen. Most men don't. I know you're a rake and have cruel tendencies, but I've never taken you for a fool, so perhaps you will listen."

Since her eyes had adjusted to the dim light, she could see him leaning against the post, still nursing his cigar. He shifted and crossed his legs. "I'm no fool."

"Helen, the leader, I've come to see her as rather blood thirsty." Kat kept her voice low on the slim chance anyone was awake across the street. "She attends to the men when they're drunk so she has an excuse for destruction of property."

"My property?"

"As the biggest, and most frequented, saloon in Dominion Falls—not to mention your whore element, you are the best option."

"And will you be joinin'?"

"I never have. I've tried to prevent them all along. I told you, I agree that temperance should be instilled, and knowledge—but I cannot stand by and watch them destroy a man's livelihood in the name of God."

"Ya know when?"

"They usually come first thing once business opens. They want an audience."

"Your friends go to Cottonwood Springs a while back?"

"Yes." She leaned on the post opposite him and mimicked his stance.

"Ruined a friend of mine's business. I ain't complainin' too much, I got his whores outta the deal. He went west for gold."

"If you don't want them to do the same to you, you'd best be prepared. I just wanted to warn you."

"I'm warned. I'll be ready for 'em."

"Good. Consider us even."

He snorted. "How's that?"

"I just saved you thousands of dollars' worth of damage. I'd say we're even for the assistance you gave me getting out of here, and sending me somewhere safe."

"That mean you ain't gonna make it right otherwise?"

"That means I won't sell myself for any debt. I'm no whore." Kat straightened her back and lifted her chin. "I choose when and with whom I lay."

In the dark she couldn't tell if he was impressed, annoyed, or anything else. When he lingered in silence, she pushed off the post and walked across the porch right past him.

She paused at the end of the porch long enough to say, "If you decide my debt is paid we will continue the discussion."

"It's repaid."

"Are you saying that to see if you can remove my pantaloons?"

"Maybe."

"I thought so." Kat turned to face him again. "If you mean it, we'll talk."

"Come in. Have a drink before you go back." There was a hint of demand in his tone, one that wasn't used to being ignored. "No charge."

"Sorry. I don't take free drinks. I'd hate to build on my debt."

"Then five cents."

She pondered the prospect of making him sweat, but truth be told, it had been months since her last coupling, and the man hadn't been very competent. "Two bits for two drinks. That's your standard, isn't it?"

"Was giving you the ladies discount." He drawled in a knowing tone. "Standard for any woman brave enough to drink in my saloon."

"Fine. Ten cents for a drink, and I'm not paying a cent less."

"Yes ma'am." He strode to the door and held it open. When she passed by, he murmured, "Ya know I don't like demandin' women, right?"

"Shame. You could use one." She went right up to the bar and sat, relieved when he turned up the one lamp still lit. At least now she could see his features. "Maybe one day you'll get one and keep her."

He snorted and almost slammed the cups on the bar. "And you'll get married one day, too."

"Touché."

"What?"

"Never mind, just pour." The second her glass was full, she tossed it back. When he filled it the second time, his eyebrow raised and she took care to be slower about picking it up. "So why Graham?"

"Just because." He slammed his drink back, and refilled his glass immediately. "I gotta have a reason why?"

"Touchy. I was just curious."

"It's a business matter."

"Of course, and my simple female mind couldn't handle it." She took a swig of her whiskey. "Fine. You choose a topic."

"I don't like talking."

"You are a sad, sad man."

Cole finished off his second whiskey and tapped the bar. "Two dimes. Then get out."

She had no idea what nerve she'd touched, but it had flared him into defensive mode and brought out the attitude he'd been rumored to have. Rather than argue, she fished two dimes out of her reticule and set them on the counter. "Good night, Cole."

"Wait." He circled the bar and grasped her neck in his strong hand. In an instant she realized she could be in over her head, rumor was one of the men in charge at the saloon had hit a whore or two.

Without realizing it, she'd held her breath, and gasped for air when her lungs grew tight. Before she could fight him off and walk away, though, he yanked her close. The kiss surprised her enough to allow him instant access to her mouth, which he plundered with fevered intensity.

Every inch of her came alive and her hesitation flew out the doors. She slid her arms around his neck and returned the kiss with equal fire.

He pulled her off the stool, her body pressed against his so she could feel his excitement pressed against her belly. She moaned and reached to tug his shirt free of his trousers. The moment her fingers brushed his flesh, he returned her moan in kind.

When he released her, he licked his swollen lips and grinned. "Your debt is repaid. Ya still wanna leave?"

"Hell no."

\* \* \* \*

The next morning, Kat woke deliciously sore. She hadn't had this many aches in all the right places since her first encounters with Patrick. Cole lived up to his reputation, and more. He'd been voracious, like an animal in only the best way.

She was, however, rather surprised that he still lay beside her. If anything, she'd expected him to high-tail it out of the room once their enjoyment was complete. He'd receive no complaint from her for remaining; she enjoyed the feeling of his strong, hard body against hers.

Of course, she held no grand romantic illusions about their current situation. There was no way the man currently moving in for another round would ever be more than a conquest for her, or she for him. Of course, that didn't mean she couldn't enjoy every second, and she certainly intended to.

Unfortunately, a crash outside the room startled them both to sitting and pulled Cole's marvelously skilled wandering hands from her flesh.

"Damn," he cursed. "Was hopin' for a better start to the day."

"You're not the only one," she agreed. After a yawn, she stretched until her back curved. Another crash drew their gazes to the door. "What in heaven is that?"

"I'm gonna find out. Ain't your ladies already is it?"

"I wouldn't know. What time is it?"

"Dunno."

She sighed and rose, well aware his gaze remained on her even as he got his trousers back on. Perhaps later she'd take further advantage, or maybe not if he was going to laugh at her. "What is so funny?"

"Ya look like a wild woman, all them curls stickin' out everywhere."

"Oh, drat." She set her hands on her head, laughing with him. "Happens every time they're unleashed. You pulled out my tie early on in the evening. I must look a fright."

"Ya do." He grinned, but it faded when the next crash came on loud with the distinct crack of wood. "I ain't open; thought you said they wouldn't attack."

"They usually don't!" Kat snatched the sheet and wrapped it around herself as she raced out behind him.

Sure enough, the ladies of the temperance league were streaming in through the busted door. Helen stood proud at the front with her hatchet.

Kat gasped. "Helen! What are you doing attacking with hatchets at this hour?"

Helen's eyes widened and the hatchet slipped from her hand. "Katherine, what are you doing?"

Cole strode toward the woman, and moved fast enough to take Helen's hatchet before she could recover from her shock to grab it herself. "Get outta my saloon."

"No." Without her hatchet, Helen's voice wavered.

"I said," Cole hefted the hatchet, "get outta my saloon."

Helen backed up a step, which brought an inappropriate giggle out of Kat. When Helen glared at her, Kat only shrugged. "You won't win this time. If you try to keep on, I'll get every man on the street to abandon his wagon and come help Cole haul every one of you out of here."

"You defend this solicitor of sin?" Helen's nose wrinkled. "Then again, you gave into his devilish ways. You should be ashamed."

"Oh, do stop putting on such false airs. I know you've made time with men on our trip. You scream when you lie with them, we all know it." Kat scooted closer to Cole's side. "And Cole may not be a good man-"

Cole snorted and dropped the hatchet to his shoulder. "That so?"

"But he's not the devil, either. He's supplying exactly what the men would get elsewhere in other more devious ways if no saloons existed." Kat glanced at Cole out of the corner of her eye and offered him a wink.

"She's making stories to divert us from our task! She wouldn't walk into the street in nothing but a sheet." Helen's voice took on a desperate shrill. "Onward."

Kat pushed her way past Helen toward the door. Most of the ladies moved out of her way, but Lottie remained in the broken doorway, hatchet in hand. Kat stood in front of the young woman without fear. "You'd best move, or I'll tell Helen all about what happened in Kansas. I doubt you'll be welcome in a world of temperance, then."

Lottie paled, her freckles standing out in stark relief at the change. When the ladies had been camped out at their counterparts' bedside, and Kat had been helping Bess, Lottie had stolen away from the group. Kat alone knew Lottie had been at a brothel with a woman, and had been so drunk Kat had to retrieve her and sober her up to return her to the hospital for vigil.

Through several queries from the others about what happened in Kansas, Lottie held her ground. Then she dropped her eyes and shook her head. "We should go. We cannot change things here."

"She's right, Helen." Kat turned back to the leader, intentionally flashing her leg as she did. "I guarantee that if you break anything more than that door, I will get a lawyer and make sure you stay in jail. The word of God won't help you there."

Cole pushed Helen toward the door. "Move. You don't wanna know what I'll do if ya try to stay."

"What's going on in here?" Graham barreled in, knocking over Lottie in the process. "What're all these—well, hello there Kathy."

"You do not have permission to call me that." Kat glared her annoyance right at Graham. "And these women thought they'd take some time to destroy the bar."

"Graham." Cole tossed the hatchet at the bulky man. "Hold that. Any of 'em move, do what ya need to."

Kat jumped back when Cole grabbed Helen and flung her over his shoulder. Helen's shriek must have startled the whores into action, because they came spilling out of the back. Kat's own curiosity couldn't be sated, so she darted to the window and threw open the shutters when Cole burst through the broken door.

As he carried Helen to the trough, Kat almost dropped her sheet trying to cover her laughter. "Oh, he isn't!"

The women gathered around the shutters, exclamations and protests wrenching the morning air. Laughter from the whores interrupted the indignation, and Kat had to join the whores at the large splash of water that flew over the edge of the trough. "He did!"

The ladies dropped their hatchets on their rush outside to tend to Helen. As a crowd gathered outside and Graham moved to pick up the hatchets, Kat rushed back to the room she'd shared with Cole the night before.

She was halfway dressed when the door opened and shut again. With her hands on her buttons, she froze. "Cole?"

"Yeah. Just came to find my damn shirt."

"I think that came off in the other room." Kat turned to face him as she buttoned the last button. "Can't remember where I threw it, though."

"Shame. Guess I don't wear a shirt when I go find Hammy about fixin' my damn door. Crazy loons, every one of them."

Kat chuckled. "You'll simultaneously embarrass and thrill every woman you pass."

"You won't be ashamed."

"If I were a hypocrite I would pretend, but I won't."

He leaned against the wall when she tried to tame her hair down. "You ain't gettin' any ideas, are ya?"

"Ideas?" She quirked a brow, but dropped it quickly in the battle with her hair. "If you're asking if I'm going to get all moony eyed over you, the answer is no. I had fun last night and sure wouldn't mind doing it again, but I have no aspirations of turning you into a good man who does right with the strength of a good woman."

"Ya wanna again? Now?"

"As romantic as your suggestion is, I need to get to the Silver Saddle and get my things moved out." Kat wouldn't admit she actually would right then. Last thing he needed was to think he held any power or sway over her. "Perhaps another day, if I'm feeling peckish."

"Fair enough."

"Thank you, by the way. It's been a while since I've been around a man that could handle a woman the right way. I needed that."

"Glad I could help."

"I'm glad you could, too."

\* \* \* \*

Kat hovered at the top of the stairs, staring at her current landlord, of sorts, Cora Turner. Cora had been kind enough to let Kat keep a room, and had refused payment. So instead, Kat got to enjoy good food, good company, and see a happy family in motion. It had been years since she'd been around such a thing as a happy family.

At the bottom of the stairs Cora stood at a table chopping vegetables to dump in the pot beside her. The sweet smell of blackberry pie filled the air, and Cora hummed as she worked. Her dark hair was done up in a loose knot with a few strays flying free. A young boy with dark curls darted in and around her skirts and the table, seemingly unnoticed by her as she continued her work

She turned her head and smiled at Kat as she descended the stairs. "There you are, you lie-a-bed. You're off to an awful late start today."

"Honestly, I was reading and enjoying the quiet." Kat grinned and snatched the little boy on his next race around Cora's skirts. "What are you up to, Isaac? Are you pestering your Mama?"

Isaac blew a raspberry and tried to flip right out of Kat's arms.

Kat chuckled and set the boy down to resume his racing. In the past week she'd continued to indulge in multiple pleasurable evenings with Cole. Word had spread like wildfire through the town, helped along by Graham, she was sure.

The rumors and buzz had created some ignorant comments and judgment from certain members of the town, but Kat ignored them as always. To her credit, after an initial scolding and warning to think about what she was doing, Cora still treated Kat the same as she had when she'd offered her a room.

"Sorry I missed breakfast, but is that blackberry pie I smell?" Kat popped a piece of carrot in her mouth.

"Sure is. You planning on being here for lunch?" Cora kept chopping, her knife working through the vegetables with quick efficient movements despite her laughing toddler. "Beef stew and fried chicken are on the menu."

"Cora, I'm telling you—putting the restaurant into your general store was a stroke of genius. I wouldn't miss your stew for anything." Kat gave her friend a half-hug so as to not interrupt her work. "But if I'm going to be back here, I have a few errands to run first."

"Don't miss another meal." Cora scolded with knife in hand. "I won't have a starving boarder on my watch."

"Promise. I might even have two slices of pie."

"Glutton."

Kat didn't bother denying, just waved over her shoulder as she ran from the store. Halfway down the steps, she stopped. The stagecoach was back in town, which meant the ladies were leaving.

After Helen's embarrassing dumping in the horse trough, they'd become virtual hermits in Martha's boarding house. No one had seen hide nor tail of them, even at church.

Moments later Helen came around the coach, and stopped when she spotted Kat. Helen's eyes narrowed and she lifted her nose in the air before she flounced to the coach.

Kat snorted and hopped down the rest of the stairs to head down the street. Several buildings away Lottie paced back and forth, casting an occasional glance toward the stagecoach. When she spotted Kat, Lottie scrambled to change her footing and head Kat's direction. "Kat."

At the use of her preferred name, Kat lifted a brow. Lottie hadn't ever bothered to use the name she preferred, and Kat was sure it was done to annoy her. Kat pursed her lips and slowed to meet her. "Yes?"

"You aren't going to tell, are you?"

Kat sagged and shook her head. "Selfish thoughts as always, I see. What purpose would me telling anyone do? It was a threat, one that worked."

"Good. I've got nowhere else to go."

"I'm sure you'd find somewhere if you stopped pretending." Kat set her hand on Lottie's shoulder. "Take care of yourself. You're not a bad person, but you'll be one if you keep on the path you're on."

Lottie's eyes glistened with tears, but not one fell. She tore her gaze away. "I'd best be off. Farewell, Kat."

"Farewell. Be careful." Kat sighed as Lottie took off toward the coach. She spared a moment of concern over where the young woman would end up, but then let it drop. There were a lot of things she could change, Lottie was no longer one of them.

With a shrug, Kat turned and resumed her path down the boardwalk. She wanted to stop the telegraph office and send word to Patrick, and see if he'd sent any to her.

An elegant woman with chestnut hair done up in an elaborate knot under an equally elaborate hat stepped out of a door just ahead of Kat. The woman tugged her skirt free of a loose nail and pulled the door closed behind her.

Kat smiled in greeting. "Dr. Pearson, yes?"

"What? Oh, my. I mean, yes." Dr. Pearson tipped her head in a nod, but her gaze travelled along Kat's clothing before reaching her face. "I'm Dr. Pearson. May I help you? It's Miss Daugherty, right?"

"I prefer Kat, but yes. I was hoping to set an appointment." Kat's smile grew at the wide eyed surprise on the pretty doctor's features.

"Are you ill?"

"No, I don't believe so. I have been travelling for some time and," Kat stepped closer to drop her tone, "I enjoy the company of men from time to time, and it has been a while since I've seen a doctor. I wish to make sure I am healthy as I was when I left—and procure, perhaps, some precautionary measures."

Delicate pink lit the doctor's features, but she nodded. "I keep myself in supply as my only patients currently are Mr. Mitchell's whores."

"Now you have another. Thank you, Dr. Pearson." Kat held out her hand. "It's good to meet a woman in your field. It's high time I did."

"Thank you." Dr. Pearson shook her hand. "Would tomorrow morning suit you? I'm free, so you may pick your time."

"It would. I'll be by at ten. Thank you."

Dr. Pearson nodded and adjusted her bag.

"Now that business is concluded. Would you perhaps join me for lunch later? I do hate eating alone and Cora is busy in the kitchen." Kat smiled. "I would be fascinated to hear your story."

"No one wishes to hear that." A strong denial, but a smile teased her features.

"I do. Please, join me at noon. You'd be doing me a favor. I mean, if you don't have plans with your husband."

"No. He's out on business. I'll join you. Thank you."

"Good. I'll see you then." Kat slipped off before the doctor could come up with a viable excuse. Down the street, Kat's sister stood on the porch of the boarding house beating a rug over the hitching post.

Kat debated taking another route and avoiding her sister as she had all week, but she supposed the time to be childish was over. If she stayed in Dominion Falls for any length of time, she'd have to see Martha now and then.

With her shoulders squared, she kept going down the boardwalk.

Not surprisingly, when Martha turned her way, she ceased beating the rug and set her hands on her hips. Martha's graying hair was breaking free of her bun from the exertion of her working, and her once thin waist had expanded some inches.

Kat almost felt bad for the change her sister had undergone. Almost.

"Katherine." Martha touched her arm. "Wait."

"For what?" Kat turned toward her sister, ready for a fight. "You to tell me what a horrible person I am? Or perhaps tell Mother and drag her here?"

"I just don't believe you're thinking. To take up with a man like Cole Mitchell is a grievous mistake."

"Don't be so dramatic. I've not 'taken up' with anyone. I am enjoying Cole's company, that is all. Men do it all the time, why shouldn't a woman when she wants?"

"It's not right, or decent."

"Right? Decent? You're a fine one to talk." Kat bowed to her sister. "To Martha, the most hypocritical person in Dominion Falls."

"I beg your pardon?" Martha's nostrils flared in indignation. "I'm not a hypocrite."

"But you *are*. You, who took up with an Indian while engaged. You, who were with a good man like Daniel—and got pregnant by another man. You are a fine one to talk about what is right and decent in the world."

"You wouldn't have the faintest idea what I went through during that time." Martha gripped her rug beater. "You were a child."

"Exactly. *Was*. I nearly had to bear the consequences of your actions. However, I'm an adult now and can make my own choices." Kat stepped closer. "You've tried to become this perfect person to make up for what you did. Problem is, people hate you more now than they did then. Maybe they'd have gotten over the whole Starbird thing if you hadn't become the epitome of mother at her most uptight."

"I had to make it right," Martha whispered.

"Some things, you never can." Kat turned on her heel and strode away.

"You've never been in love, Kat!" Martha called after her, "When you are, you'll understand then."

Kat brushed off the words as desperation and rushed along the muddy street quick as she could. There were no further impediments to her arrival at the telegraph office.

Inside Norman sorted mail into boxes, his back to the door. "Be right there," he said in an acerbic tone, like he was annoyed anyone dared interrupt him from his work for a different sort of work.

She covered her mouth to hide her giggle. For some reason she found the grumpy gentleman endearing. In the week since she'd been home they'd had a few run-ins, usually right in his office. She'd become convinced his admonishments were little more than him trying to give her advice, it just happened to come in the form of scolding.

"No hurry, Norman," Kat said when she managed to stop her quiet laughter. If anything, she wanted to be nice to him. She thought maybe he was lonely after his wife had passed some years ago. An older gentleman often had few prospects once his wife was gone, and as they'd never had children, he had no one else to pester.

"Oh, it's you." He kept his back to her, slipping envelopes into boxes until the small stack was depleted. "What're you after?"

"Quite a bit, actually." She leaned on the counter with a bright grin. "Life, laughter, happiness, fun."

He grumbled and moved to his desk. "Got a wire for ya."

"Oh, good. Is it from Patrick?"

"In St. Louis, yeah." Norman set it on the counter. "What else?"

She read the wire quickly. Bess was doing well, and he was pleased she'd managed to have fun. She grinned. "First, I'd like to reply. Then, I have another request."

Norman got his pad out and wrote almost as fast as she spoke. He ticked off the words with his pencil and nodded. "That'll be two bits."

"Of course." Kat handed him the money, then set her hand on his arm. "Would you join me for supper this evening?"

He narrowed his eyes at her hand, then lifted his gaze to meet hers. "'Scuse me?"

"You aren't going deaf. You heard me."

"What're you doin'? Makin' a spectacle of yourself like ya are, and now this?"

"I'm not making a spectacle. Others are making one for me. I tried to be discreet, but people had other ideas." She pulled her hand back. "I thought I would like the company, and I thought you might as well. Forgive me, for I see I was wrong."

He shook his head. "Why Cole?"

"Well, why not? I have no delusions of love, not with him. I have yet to find a man that would make me feel that way."

"Then you are the one that needs company, not me. I had that once."

"She's been gone nine years. You must get lonely."

"No man is lonely in this town 'less he wants to be."

"Whores aren't company. They're sexual release."

"Woman like you shouldn't be talking like that."

"And yet, here I am." Kat grinned and leaned on the counter. "That's what Cole is for me, and I for him. Perhaps we'll be friends, but that has yet to happen. Please, Norman. I would love if you'd join me for supper."

"No." He turned and went back to his work. The click of the telegraph filled the office in his silence.

"If you change your mind, I'll be at Turner's. Good afternoon, Norman."

* * * *

Kat stepped onto the porch of the saloon with every intention of walking right past, but as Cole stood there, she went ahead and made a detour. "Good morning."

"Mornin'." He didn't turn from his stance of watching the passersby. Somehow, the area in front of his saloon was always free of the carts that lined every other inch of the streets, even in front of the Silver Saddle.

She leaned on the hitching post next to him. "Saw you working the horses this morning. That paint is giving you fits."

"He'll break, they all do."

"You're awful sure of yourself." At that moment, Dr. Pearson and her husband walked past. Kat nodded to them both before continuing, "In many things. Some that perhaps you shouldn't be."

"I know what I'm good at." His lips curved up in a sexy smirk. "I'm also usually right. I was right about you."

"Dr. Pearson is no me. I had lunch with her the other day, you know. She's rather in love with her husband and quite good at her job. I see no possible scenario where you could end up right."

"It'll happen. Dunno how, but it will." He finally turned to glance at her. "Ya here for some fun?"

"Oooh, after watching you work the horses this morning that is a tempting offer, but I was just passing by. Perhaps later, if you aren't too busy."

"Graham's workin' the saloon tonight. I could squeeze in some time."

"Then perhaps I'll swing by." She winked and pushed off the hitching post. "Until later, then."

Cole gave her a nod, but then returned to watching the town. She wondered just what he saw or thought about when he stood there like that for hours. Part of her suspected there might be something deeper there, but she also knew she hadn't the patience or enough depth of feeling to draw it out.

Long ago, with Patrick, she'd learned to recognize her limits. Sometimes she failed, but in her impression of Cole, she had little doubt. This man was for pleasure or friendship, not both at once, and certainly not love. As their friendship budded, she knew the pleasure would pass, and she was fine with that.

Halfway down the street a familiar voice called her name. She turned to find Norman heading her way. Unbidden, a smile crossed her lips. "Good morning, Norman."

"Got a telegram for ya." Norman held out the paper. "Figured you'd wanna see it right away. It's from your ma."

Her hand clenched around the paper and her stomach flipped. Without reading the telegram, she scrunched it in her fist. "You figured wrong, Norman. I don't wish to see it. Not in the slightest."

"Well, someone done told her you were here."

"I suppose it was bound to happen." She tightened her grip on the telegram, but forced her smile back in place. "That was very nice of you to bring it to me, though. I mean, I do go to the office every day you could have given me the telegram then."

His weathered features darkened, but he shrugged. "Ya already came by today. I was goin' to eat anyhow, figured I'd bring it with."

"I was on my way to eat as well." She laced her arm with his even though he didn't offer. "So now you can finally join me."

"Aw, I didn't say that."

"I did." She pulled him along with her. "We're both eating, it just makes sense to not eat alone, don't you think?"

"I suppose."

"I thought you'd see it my way." She led him up the steps to Turners and into a seat. Once they'd ordered, she leaned on the table. "So, Norman. Tell me about yourself."

"Ain't nothin' to tell." He sipped his coffee and scanned the room.

"I doubt that. Where are you from?"

"Missouri."

She clenched her jaw and pondered how to break his tightlipped nature. "Missouri, what part?"

"Minnesota."

"What?" Kat's confusion dissolved into laughter when she caught a hint of a grin on Norman's face. "Care to explain?"

"Missouri was just becomin' a state 'round the time I was born. I was born in the Minnesota part of the Missouri Territory. Don't rightly remember where, there weren't no big towns near. Pa was a trapper."

"Really? So your family was isolated?" She wondered what that was like. For all her life she'd been surrounded by people.

"For a time." Norman finished off his coffee, holding it out for more when their food was brought to the table. Once his cup was refilled, he took another sip. "Pa got killed by Injuns when I was 'bout five, I think. Ma high-tailed it outta there with me right quick. Went back to Ohio with her family. I came back west soon as I was of age."

"Why?"

"I didn't like Ohio none, or my ma's family. I stopped soon as Indiana for a time to earn some more money. Thought I'd get enough to start a business in a new town. Worked in a cooper shop in Indianapolis."

"That's where you met Elizabeth, isn't it? I remember mother saying she came from there, and that she was a fine woman."

"Betsy was the best." Norman nodded in agreement. "Always real delicate, though. She had a weak heart. That's what killed her."

"I remember." Kat lowered her head in respect for his late wife. "She was always real nice, though. Gave me candies whenever I came in with mother."

"She had a soft spot for the kids. We never could have any of our own."

"You wanted children?" She smiled, doing her best not to laugh. "You always yelled at us children when we ran through."

"Ya were a brat. Spoiled."

"I suppose that's true."

"Still are."

"I would have to protest. I am a brat, but I am no longer spoiled. I worked for my money and I have done well to keep it and grow it. My friend Patrick is skilled with money, and taught me a lot."

"So why'd ya come back? Ya clearly don't wanna see your ma again, and I 'spect ya will if ya hang around much longer."

"I suspect as much myself, but I no longer care. I wanted to come home. As much as I like my life, I missed Dominion Falls." She pushed the food around her plate, no longer quite so hungry. "I've lived in a city, I've travelled the country, I thought I might try settling down."

"Gettin' a husband?"

"Oh, heavens no."

"Why not?"

"I don't care for marriage. I've seen it ruin lives. Perhaps one day if I found love I might consider it, but I haven't been so lucky."

"Marriage ain't so bad." Norman finished off his tea and cleared the rest of his plate. "I should get back to work."

"Wait." Kat patted the table when he half-rose, and smiled when he took his seat again. "I've been enjoying our meal. Don't leave yet."

"I got work to do."

"I know." She pondered a moment. "Will you join me for supper tomorrow?"

"Why?"

"I'm not sure. I like you, Norman. I just like having company for my meals."

"I suppose." He rose before she could say more, and left the store.

Kat pursed her lips and pondered her desire to learn more about the curmudgeonly old man. Perhaps she should ask Patrick, but if she sent a telegram, Norman would know what she was doing.

She slipped away from the table and hopped up the stairs to write a letter quick as she could. The mail would be along later that day if it kept to schedule, and she wanted to make sure her letter was on it to get a reply soon as possible.

* * * *

*My dearest Kat,*

*Well, you've certainly found yourself on an adventure. I'm afraid I can offer little help as to the why's of your draw to this older gentleman, but if we have learned anything, it is to not fight what our souls tell us to do.*

*Your Bess has flourished since her recovery and I have made arrangements to send her on to Chicago to the "lady" that helped you learn your trade. There she will find true anonymity and a skill to keep her away from such a man again. I only hope she learns to live as you did in the city we called home.*

*As for your gentleman, continue your friendly exchange. You have never liked a lonely soul, not even your own. If it helps ease your loneliness, then I cannot deride it.*

*And as I'm sure you'd wish to know. Pearl has moved into the home I helped her find. It's a wonderful, private, place some distance from the city. She is rather skilled at gardening and enjoys living in the quiet. I enjoy visiting when I can.*

*When you have time, tell me more about the rake you've been spending time with. He sounds like a scoundrel, one I would enjoy meeting. I do enjoy meeting another of my kind from time to time, even the rougher sorts.*

*Be well, my dear. I hope you will visit again soon.*

*Follow your soul, and your instincts. They have yet to prove you wrong.*

*All my love,*
*Patrick*

Kat folded the letter and returned it to its envelope, and then into her trunk. In the month since her letter had been sent, she'd done as Patrick had gone on to suggest. All along she'd known what he'd say; she imagined she'd sent the letter to expel the confusion of her own thoughts on the matter.

Spending more time had not eased her confusion, though. All she'd done is add to it. Turned out, she found Norman to be a dear man under his gruff exterior, and the life he'd led before he wound up in Dominion Falls was always fun to hear about.

She feared her heart was getting caught up in the mix, and that would do her no good in the end. Still, she met with him for supper or lunch several times a week. Plus her daily trips to the telegraph office for her regular exchanges with Patrick were lasting longer every time.

With a sigh, she left her room to head toward the saloon. This time around, she was not taking advantage of the ever-intense bedding of Cole. No, she'd asked him to teach her poker. Living in the city had left her rarely without something to do, but now that she was back home, she was itching for new ways to occupy her time.

Without a home of her own to keep or a job, she had too much free time. If she didn't figure out something to do with her time she was likely to become an idle gossip, and she certainly didn't want that.

Cole's voice interrupted her musing. "You're late."

"And you're drunk."

"Not drunk. Drinkin'." Cole winked and tipped back his glass of whiskey. "Sit, I got some of that confounded brandy for ya, and you're gonna drink it."

"Aren't you grumpy today?" Kat took a seat and poured herself a glass of brandy. "What crawled up your britches?"

"Damn Graham." After he poured another glass for himself, Cole set about shuffling the cards. "Now, to play poker—"

"What did Graham do?" Kat asked at the same time as he launched into his explanation. She grinned. "Oh, sorry. You were going to explain poker. Do you have some paper I can take notes on?"

"Think ya can't remember?"

"I'd rather be safe than sorry. Especially playing with sharp like yourself, I'd like to hedge my bets."

"Iris, get'er the pad Graham keeps back there." He resumed shuffling while the whore brought Kat the pad. Once Iris was lounging at a nearby table in an unseemly position, glaring at Kat, Cole started dealing.

Kat ignored the whore and focused on Cole's explanation of the game. The man didn't bother to speak slowly, so she wrote down the relevant points quick as possible until they were able to actually sit back and begin a true hand.

Though she felt she caught on quickly, Cole only laughed at her inability to bluff. She tried to restrain her features and managed to make it through a whole hand without him laughing at her. Once they settled into a good game, she glanced at her sheet to check her hand against the list to make sure she remembered how good a royal flush was.

"So what's the deal with you and the old man?"

Kat blinked and did a double take. The question came out of the blue, and while she wasn't offended by it, she didn't feel it was a topic for them as lovers. Even worse, the whore now leaned forward eagerly in her chair, ripe for gossip. Kat pursed her lips and shook her head.

"Aww, don't wanna talk about it?"

"I prefer to discuss personal matters with friends." After another pointed glance toward Iris, Kat tossed another coin on the table to raise the bet.

Cole flicked his hand toward the door and whistled at Iris. "Get on out there and stir up some business. Go on, get."

Iris planted her feet on the floor and rose. She glared at Kat, then spun toward the door. The whore flounced out the door, grumbling under her breath the whole way.

"So spill."

"There's nothing to spill. I'm afraid you offended your favorite whore over nothing." Kat leaned back in her seat and grinned.

"She ain't my favorite. Just acts like she is 'cause she's been here longest. I don't believe ya. Ya been leadin' around Norman on a leash lately."

"I am doing no such thing!" She narrowed her eyes when he chuckled. "I have enjoyed some meals with him, and a few walks. You know, he's rather interesting when you take the time to get to know him."

"He's old."

"So?" She turned her cards down when Cole finally met her bet. "Royal flush."

"Damn. Shouldn'ta taught ya."

"I know you hate losing, but it's one game. I'm sure there's time to make your money back. Let's go again."

"I just don't get it."

"You don't have to." Kat sighed when he continued shuffling rather than deal. "I enjoy his company. Turns out Norman has led an interesting life when you take a moment to hear it—and I mean hear it, not pour him drinks to shut him up."

"I don't."

"You do."

He shrugged.

"I hate to break it to you."

"What?"

"By having this conversation, teaching me cards, we're tipping the scale toward friends. We may have to cease our scandalous activities if this keeps up. I don't mix friendship with sex."

"Damn. Shoulda kept my mouth shut."

"Told you so."

\* \* \* \*

Kat breezed into the telegraph office. "Good morning, Norman."

"Mornin', Kat." Over the course of the past few weeks, Norman's customary gruff greetings had warmed. "How are ya today?"

"I'm marvelous. How about yourself? Did my telegram come?"

"Like clockwork. Soon as I opened. Does this Patrick not have a job or nothin'?" Norman frowned at the telegram as he pushed it over the counter.

"Of course he does. I'm certain he writes it before he leaves and has Loren send it soon as you open. He does have a telegraph in his house."

"Fancy Nancy."

"Norman," Kat chided. "He is my friend, and a good one."

"Like Cole?"

"No. Cole just started being my friend. Before that we were merely coupling. Now we're becoming friends, and the sex will cease soon enough."

He grunted and turned away.

Rather than try to comprehend the meaning behind his grunt, Kat turned her attention to the wire in her hand. As usual, Patrick had little to report. After all, they now wired almost daily. She suspected he was rather bored and lonely now that Pearl had gone to Indiana to visit the one sister she still spoke to.

Once she'd written a quick reply and set the coins on the counter, she tapped Norman's shoulder. "I guess that'll be all."

"What're ya off doin' today?"

"I hadn't any plans set."

"I got somethin' I wanna show ya."

Kat couldn't conceal her shock at the statement, and had to physically make her mouth close. She blinked rapidly and shook her head. "What? I mean, certainly. What is it?"

"We gotta walk. That's if'n ya don't mind."

"No. I don't mind at all. What about the office?"

Norman tapped the knob on the telegraph key in rapid, distinct clicks. When he straightened, he gave her a short nod and indicated to the door. "It's taken care of."

"Well, then." Kat took his offered arm. Butterflies sprang to life in her stomach, fluttering and flipping around with nervous anticipation. For the first time she hadn't initiated their interaction. Perhaps Norman was softening to her after all.

Norman, never one for chatter, didn't say much as he led her away from town. They walked down the road that led to the outer settlements, only pausing so they could both stand where the railroad tracks would pass and look toward the mountains where they'd come through eventually.

They hadn't gone quite a quarter of a mile before the small homestead came into view. She remembered the homestead being half-finished, devoid of life, before she'd left Dominion Falls. She couldn't even remember who'd been building it then, but she had noticed when she moved back that it had come to life, although it still seemed to be without an occupant.

Someone had finished the home finally, and painted it a cheery yellow. Though the homestead was empty, chair perched on the small porch, just waiting for occupants. She could picture the flower boxes on the window full of life, along with the house.

Much to Kat's surprise, Norman slowed to a stop in front of the small home.

"Norman?"

"I was buildin' it for Betsy, then she up and died."

She gasped and eyed the house. "I'd forgotten it was yours. You just left it to rot after she passed. When I left there was no porch or windows. Did someone buy it?"

"Nah. Lots of promises I didn't keep to Betsy. Few years ago I figured I'd finish one promise and fixed it up real nice. Thought I might sell it, but ain't been able to let it go."

"Understandable. I'm sure Elizabeth would have loved it. I remember she wore yellow all the time."

"Was her favorite color. But she's gone now. It's time to let go, I s'pose."

"Only you can know if it's time."

"Thought maybe you'd wanna live here so's you can get outta Cora's place, I mean."

"What?" Kat dropped her hand from his arm and took a step back.

"I'd rent it to ya, if ya want. If not, I'll probably sell it."

"I couldn't live in Betsy's house. It's a lovely gesture, and I appreciate the kindness, but it wouldn't be right, me living there what with you ready to move on…"

"I reckon I am. Been nine years, after all." He cleared his throat and turned his back on the house. When he offered his arm again, she didn't hesitate to take it. As they walked, this time he spoke, "So ya said you lived in Chicago for a time?"

"I did. Rather enjoyed my life there, right up until the end."

"Miss it any?"

"Some. I miss Patrick, but he's not there any longer, as you know. I miss Delphie terribly, but she just passed a little over a year ago so it will take time. I think what I miss most is this little confectionary on Green Street had a delightful candy called a praline."

"A what?"

She laughed. "That's what I said. The woman that made them, she came from New Orleans and ordered in pecans just for these candies. They're pure heaven."

"And that's what you miss?"

"Outside of my friends, yes. Chicago was just a place. I can live just about anywhere once I decide to stay."

"Huh." He kept his pace slow. "And are ya gonna stay here?"

"Can't say for certain, but it's looking promising."

\* \* \* \*

Half the town bustled around the supply wagon before it came to a full stop. Kat hid her laughter behind her hand as Norman hollered at everyone and bullied his way through for the mail bag.

"You'd think we hadn't had a supply wagon in weeks." Cora leaned on the railing next to Kat. "I expect this in the middle of winter, but today it's a surprise."

"I heard Grover Star was getting in more mining supplies today. Apparently the fire last week destroyed a lot of men's tools. He made the mistake of offering a discount to those that paid ahead." Kat shook her head. "Now they're all trying to claim in advance. I don't think Kelly's going to get anywhere near that wagon until they're done."

"He's not trying. My husband is foolishly trying to play peacekeeper since we haven't a sheriff to do the job." Cora shrugged. "Norman, however, was pretty hard pressed to get to that mail bag. Wonder what he's after."

"I have no idea." It was curious, especially as Norman still stood by the wagon, digging through the bag. She'd learned it was his habit to not let anyone near the bag until he'd gotten it to his office and organized, so this was out of character to say the least. "It's certainly odd to see."

"He looks like a child eying our candy display to pick just the right gum drop."

Kat laughed. "That's exactly what he looks like. Makes him look twenty years younger."

"Not that such a thing seems to matter to you."

"Of course not."

"I must say, it's been nice to see Norman less surly lately. I think you've had something to do with that."

"I wouldn't begin to claim such a thing." Kat fought the urge to fidget. "I am merely being nice."

"You care for him."

Kat didn't have time to protest, even if she could've. Norman himself walked up wearing the closest thing to a grin she'd ever seen on his face. Unable to stop her own smile, she nodded her head. "Norman."

"This came for ya." He set a box in her hand, then turned and strode back down the steps without another word.

"What in the world?" Kat glanced at Cora before turning her attention to the small box in her hands. The plain brown paper had Norman's name on it, and an address in Chicago as the source. "Oh, heavens. No, he didn't, did he?"

"He didn't what?" Cora leaned closer. "Why did he give that to you?"

Kat peeled away the string and tore open the brown paper. Within moments she had the box inside open, and six pralines sat nestled inside. Her heart melted, and she set her hand on her chest to ease the sudden rapid beat within. "Oh, he did. What a dear man."

"Might I ask what those are?" Cora peeked in the box. "Is that candy?"

"They're pralines. From a little confectionery in Chicago I used to enjoy. We talked about it weeks ago. I didn't expect this." She plucked one from the box and held it out to Cora. "Try one. I bet you could replicate them, you'd just need to order the nuts."

"Thank you." Cora took a bite, and immediately groaned. "Very good."

"Aren't they?" Kat took a bite of hers, letting the candy melt smoothly over her tongue before she bit into the pecan. When she spoke, it was around the candy. "Will you set this in my room? I need to go thank him."

"Of course. Would you mind if—"

"Go ahead and take another. I don't mind sharing." Kat hopped down the steps and around the crowd that still hung around the supply wagon. Kelly had things under control now, but the men were taking their sweet time listening to him and Grover.

She hopped up on the boardwalk and brushed the dust from her pantaloons. Lately she'd noticed them getting tight, no doubt thanks to Cora's robust meals.

The last thing she needed was to be eating in between meals, but she'd never turn down a praline. She couldn't believe that Norman had gotten her favorite candy just because she'd said she missed it. Such a kind gesture had her almost skipping down the street until a shrill whistle pulled her to a stop.

Across the street Cole curled his finger to call her close.

She acquiesced only because her mood was already in a good place. A few feet away she paused. "Cole, was there something I could do for you?"

"You're actin' strange. What's that?" Cole pointed to the praline.

"Candy. Norman had it shipped in from Chicago for me."

"He did, did he?"

"Mm-hmm." She took another bite and sighed.

"We're done, ain't we?"

"I'm afraid so. It was marvelously fun, though. Still friends?"

He chuckled. "Don't know any woman that would want to."

"Now you do. Shall we play poker tomorrow?"

"Ya got a deal."

Kat nodded and turned on her heel, popping the last bit of candy in her mouth as she headed for the telegraph office. She wiped her sticky fingers on her pants before she pushed open the door.

Thankfully the office was empty, save for Norman sorting his mail with the back to the door. "Gimme a minute," he spoke in a gruff tone.

She walked for the half door that separated the two areas of the store, and pushed through without hesitation. Before he could fully turn to protest, she flew across the room and planted a kiss on his lips.

He grunted in surprise, but when her arms went around his neck, he slid his hands around her waist. When she pulled back, he frowned. "Ya ain't supposed to be back here."

"Too bad, you dear sweet man." She kissed him again.

"Aw, shucks. Ya better stop that."

"I'm afraid you're rather stuck with me now, Norman."

\* \* \* \*

True to her word, Kat had spent all day and night with Norman, and continued the trend for a full week. Every day after he insisted on needing to work, she'd return to Cora's to freshen up and write a letter to Patrick. Then she'd play a few rounds of cards with Cole before returning to Norman's.

As he tapped on the telegraph key, she watched in fascination. The return clicks came so fast, she couldn't begin to understand what they said. "How do you do that?"

He finished writing, tapped the key a few more times, then glanced at her. "Just do. Ya gotta sit and listen and it's easy."

"But it's so fast, and all those clicks run together."

"Here." He pulled down a book from the shelf. "Look at that."

"Are you trying to put me off?"

"No. Look at it."

"Fine." She pulled open the book, and on the first two pages were the letters of the alphabet with dots and lines above each. "Oh."

"That's the code. If ya memorize it, I'll teach ya more."

"So I could send a wire directly to Patrick if I wished."

"That's right."

"Oh goodness. How fun." She sat back and began to study the letters carefully. Around her, Norman continued to work, and part of her wondered if he was feeling triumphant that he'd managed to hush her for some time.

In the end, the studying was tough work, but made the time go by fast. Before she knew it, Norman was standing in front of her. "Ya know, you're makin' people talk stayin' here and still goin' to Cole's."

"Are you concerned about Cole? Jealous, maybe?" His lack of answer made her lower the book and lift her gaze to his. "Cole and I are friends alone. He has whores to keep him occupied. We had fun, I won't lie, but I am not lying with him any longer. I wouldn't do that to you."

"Good."

"As far as people talking goes, they'll do that anyhow. You'll have to trust me, take me at my word. I am friends with Cole same as you are. We drink and play cards, but no more, not any longer."

"I ain't too happy about it, but I guess." He jerked his head to the door. "Supper time, if ya want."

At the mere mention of food, her stomach growled. "Apparently I do." She set aside the book and rose. After they'd left and he'd locked the door behind them, she laced her arm with his.

"That ain't all they're sayin'."

"Of course it isn't." She knew the rumors and talk bothered him. She wished it didn't, she wished he could let it go. However, she also knew he found some of her behavior and beliefs to forward and improper.

"With ya practically living under my roof and all…"

"Norman, you know I don't wish to get married or anything akin to that. I don't mind practically living under your roof and keeping your company, but I don't care for marriage. I've seen what it can do to people."

"It didn't do nothin' bad to Betsy and me."

"True, but I'm not Betsy. You've known that all along. Please, can't we just enjoy each other and be together? Why must we make this into a marriage? It could ruin everything if we did."

"Or make it better."

"I say we leave the subject for now. Revisit in in six months time. Please, don't push me." Kat paused in her tracks and turned to face him. "I have grown to care for you a great deal, and I don't wish to lose that. Can you accept that I don't wish for marriage?"

Norman grumbled and shrugged. "I s'pose."

Kat kissed him on the cheek. "Thank you, Norman."

"Oh, stop that." He brushed at his cheek before he offered his arm again. "Makin' me look a fool, ya are."

"But I'm also keeping you quite happy." She started with him toward Turner's again. "Contentedness isn't something to just shrug off. I rather enjoy it. I think, despite your protests, you do as well."

"Ya might be right."

"Of course I am. Allow yourself to be happy, Norman. You never know how long that will last."

\* \* \* \*

Kat knocked on the clinic door, entering when Caroline beckoned her in.

Caroline kept working on the papers in front of her. "Good morning, Kat. I wasn't expecting you, did we have plans to dine again?"

"No." Kat sat in the seat across from the doctor, for once relieved that the town still wanted little to do with a woman doctor. At least she had the privacy for the conversation. "I actually hoped you might have time to see me. In a medical sense."

"What?" Caroline closed her folder and met Kat's gaze. "I just did an exam four months ago."

"I'm aware. I have an issue, though." Kat chewed her lip and stared at her hands. "At first I thought I was just eating too much of Cora's delicious food and not doing enough actual work. My pantaloons were just a bit tight, and nothing else unusual was occurring."

"And now?"

"I realized I missed my monthly a few weeks back, and the one before that was—unusual."

"Unusual?"

"I wasn't afflicted as long as usual, in fact it was barely a day in length. I didn't pay it much mind at first."

"I know you're cautious in your activities. You still come to me for your protective measures, and Cole keeps his own." Caroline rose and gestured to the back.

"And we both used them faithfully. With Norman, I do as well." Kat rose to follow the doctor to an exam room. "That's why I paid it little mind at first. It wasn't until I realized I was coming up on a full month being with Norman that I even managed to think about it deeper."

"We'll see what is going on, perhaps your concern is unfounded."

"Perhaps." Kat prepped for her exam in silence, and she was glad Caroline didn't push the matter. If this were true, she couldn't remain in Dominion Falls now. Cole wouldn't lay claim to a child and Norman…

Kat closed her eyes to ward off the rising worry of Norman's reaction. If she were honest with herself, she had begun to fall in love with Norman. Even Patrick, as far away as he was, knew it. She couldn't deny it, but she also couldn't disrupt his life with a child that wasn't his.

Only thing it would do was upset him, and worse, make him more convinced they needed to marry.

"Katherine," Caroline said quietly, setting her hand on Kat's knee. "I hate to confirm your worries, but you are with child."

Kat let out a long, deep breath she hadn't realized she was holding. "Oh dear."

"Why don't you get dressed and we'll talk in my office."

"No. I mean, yes I'll get dressed, but I need to think on this for a while. Sorry, Caroline. I need to be alone with my thoughts."

"All right. If you need anything at all, please let me know." Caroline squeezed Kat's shoulder and slipped from the room.

Once dressed, Kat sat on the exam table and tried to collect her thoughts. She was going to have a child. Part of her was over the moon at the thought of having a baby of her own. Without plans for marriage, this was rather serendipitous; even if the timing couldn't have been worse.

Kat slid off the table and left the clinic by the back door. A nice long walk was her best bet. Anything to get her thoughts in agreement with her heart.

The last thing she wanted to do was leave Norman; she'd just managed to admit her feelings. However, she would have a child.

She set her hand over her abdomen and smiled. "A child."

There was no telling how long it would be until she had no choice but to leave. Until then, should she linger or leave before it became too painful not to?

With all the questions swirling in her head, the only one she didn't have was whether she would raise the child or not. Without a doubt, she would have this child and raise it, and she didn't need to be married to do so.

However, she couldn't do so alone.

Her biggest concern now was how to tell Patrick. Clearly, she couldn't send a telegraph. If she'd learned the procedure properly she'd be able to do so herself, but Norman was still teaching her.

Oh, Norman. Kat sank to sit on a stump in the meadow outside of town. How could she leave the life she'd just become accustomed to? How could she leave Norman? If she was fully honest, she wasn't just beginning to love him, she already did. That didn't mean she was any more willing to get married.

Perhaps she didn't have to leave him completely. Once the child was born, she could return for visits. Until then, Patrick had a telegraph in his house. Communication wouldn't be impossible.

The thought of leaving Dominion Falls again broke her heart, but she knew what she had to do.

\* \* \* \*

Norman's relaxed demeanor had faded into harsh lines and a clenched fist. He worked his thumb in and out of his fist, staring at the tabletop between them. "Ya can't be serious. Ya said ya were stayin'."

"I said I was considering it." Kat reached over to set her hand on his. The tea she'd poured for them had gone cold in his lengthy silence. "If anything could have made me stay, it would be you."

"Then stay."

"I wish I could. This is an opportunity I can't let pass, though." As luck would have it, Patrick's next wire to her included a message from Pearl. The suffrage league was growing and had requested her presence. "If I can make a difference, I must."

"Ain't nothin' gonna change." He pulled his hand away.

"But maybe it will. I must try. Plus, I'll be able to visit. This isn't like your work here. Once I'm established again, I'll be able to visit."

"Visit. Hmph." He folded his arms across his chest. "That ain't what I wanted."

"Oh, Norman. Are you going to say it again?"

"I thought with time, maybe…"

"Time won't change my opinions on marriage any more than distance will change my feelings for you. I'll be back. Often as I can."

"If you're goin', just go. I ain't gonna play no games."

"Sure. When the games are yours toward the purpose of marriage, they're just fine. When they're mine toward the purpose of spending time with the man who has come to mean much to me, heaven forbid." She rose. "I don't leave for three days. I do hope that you'll soften your opinions before then."

His jaw worked back and forth, and he kept his arms clasped against him. Not once did his hard gaze waver from the cold tea in front of him.

She set her hand on his shoulder and leaned down to kiss the top of his head. "I'm truly sorry. This is something I must do. One day, I will return to Dominion Falls and stay. The timing just wasn't right this time around."

When he didn't speak, she left the telegraph office by the back door. Her heart was heavy and her feet dragged along the dirt road. Much as she knew what she needed to do, the execution of that act was far more painful in reality.

At the very least, she knew her secret would be safe. Caroline wouldn't tell, as Kat's doctor she couldn't, but she also understood why Kat didn't want Cole to know. She was a passing fancy, a fun diversion, but Cole didn't do family. The same way Kat herself didn't do marriage.

"What a tangled web," she muttered. In the two weeks since she'd learned of her situation, Kat had been delaying the inevitable as long as she could. The time had come to leave, and so she'd managed to procure a ticket on the next stage, which was when she knew she'd have to tell Norman, rather than let him see it on the passenger manifest.

Cora's voice interrupted her thoughts. "Kat. These were dropped off for you."

Kat grabbed the paper wrapped parcels with a whispered thank you.

"Are you all right?" Cora stepped closer and wrapped an arm around her shoulders.

"I'm fine. I just let Norman know I'll be leaving on the next stage. An opportunity has come up that I must act on." Kat sighed and clutched the packages close. "I'm afraid he didn't take it well."

"I imagine he didn't. This is awful sudden. Are you sure you can't stay?"

"I'm quite certain. Believe me, I wish I could, but this is something I must do."

"You'll be missed."

"And I'll miss Dominion Falls." Once again she was leaving because of forces out of her control. Perhaps one day those forces would bring her back. She returned Cora's half-hug before disentangling herself and darting up the stairs.

The packages turned out to be the pants she'd had tailored, but she didn't have the heart to try them on. Instead, she set them in her trunk.

She sat on her bed with a sigh and looked out the small window over the town. "I'm sorry, Norman. The truth would be harder to take. One day, maybe, it'll be time to tell. One day, maybe, I'll come back for good."

\* \* \* \*

The journey had been long and exhausting. Every inch of Kat's body ached, and she only wanted to crawl into the soft bed she knew would be waiting on her. Unfortunately, one thing impeded her path to that bed.

Or rather, one person.

She hadn't dared to message ahead that she was leaving, although she suspected Norman might have said something to cease the influx of telegrams. Of course, she wouldn't know, because Norman hadn't softened one iota in the time she'd been in Dominion Falls. There'd been no loving farewell, no more requests to stay. The stubborn man would hold onto his grudge until heaven knew when.

"For at least a year, until I can safely travel again. Right, little one?" She set her hand on her belly and fought off a yawn as the carriage slowed to a stop. When the driver opened the door, she accepted his help out of the carriage, but didn't wait for him to get her bags before rushing up the walk to the door.

Much to her surprise Patrick opened the door before she'd even knocked. He lifted a brow high enough to disappear under his currently unruly hair. "There you are. You had me worried."

"Patrick. I was hoping—perhaps I might stay here a while."

"You're always welcome, your room is prepared for you, but you know I must ask why. What happened? You were happy, and dare I say, in love?"

"You could dare, but as it didn't end well I'd rather you didn't." She accepted his help inside, and offered a wave to the butler, Loren as he passed to handle her bags. On the way to the parlor, she said little, but once she was seated the words spilled out. "I'm with child. No, it's not Norman's, it's Cole's."

"Oh, he wouldn't care for that."

"No, he wouldn't. Norman wouldn't, either. He'd say he's too old to raise a child. He'd certainly not care for the fact that my child is Cole's. I have to say, Pearl's message came at just the right time."

Patrick sighed and set his hand on hers. "Are you all right?"

"I don't know. The way Norman and I parted, I don't think he'll ever forgive me."

"He's the one that told me you'd left and when to expect you." He offered a weak smile. "He's also the one that has been concerned that you didn't arrive sooner."

"My train was delayed. Another up the line had trouble we had to wait on. It caused us to be sitting there a full extra day." She felt a flutter of hope bloom in her chest. "He was worried?"

"Yes."

"I suppose there's hope, then."

"There always is. Now, what are we going to do about this child?"

"What do you expect we're going to do? I'm going to raise it, it is my child. I imagine Uncle Patrick is going to be spoiling the thing until it is rotten."

"Me?"

"Yes, you."

"I do enjoy the sound of that. Uncle Patrick." He grinned. "Come. We'll have Loren move your things to the room next to mine. It has an adjoining bedroom you can use for the baby. Oh, and we'll have to start looking for a governess now."

"I don't require a governess."

"Of course you don't; it's for the child."

"You are going to spoil him."

"Or her. And yes, I am."

# Home

**Five Years Later**

Kat had returned to Dominion Falls for another visit. After
Cindy had been born, she'd come back at least twice a year to
visit. This time, something was different.

Even Patrick, as cool and collected as he usually was, had
reservations about her departure this time. At the train station
he'd held Cindy's hand and tried to convince Kat to stay. He
had told her something this time made him think she wouldn't
come back, except to get Cindy.

It was ridiculous, of course. Nothing had changed. She still
didn't want to get married, and the longer she stayed in
Dominion Falls on each visit, the more Norman talked about her
staying on and marriage all over again.

From her first return visit, Norman had been too happy to
see her to remain upset with her. She'd been just as happy to see
him. Every return visit was a treasure, but they all only lasted a
month—six weeks at most—she had a daughter to return to,
after all.

The only thing distinctly different this visit was the buzz
around town about some woman that had taken up with Cole,
much as Kat had done years ago. Norman had regaled Kat with
stories of the woman's amnesia and the mystery around her. Of
course, the buckets of scandal the woman had managed to cause
had the old biddy's buzzing with all the gossip. Truth be told,
the woman sounded right up Kat's alley.

While that was interesting enough, Kat had also caught a
glimpse of Graham Cooke with a Chinese woman. She'd been
so amused by the idea of the large buffoon coupling with the
miniscule Linh Moon, she'd made the mistake of joking about
it to Hammy. Of course, from there word had spread like
wildfire and left the mess in front of her.

Shouted words came from inside the saloon, and the crowd outside leaned in to hear Graham shout at the blond woman that had followed none other than Sheriff David Schaffer and a handsome deputy inside. Kat made her way through the crowd, ignoring the destroyed property outside the entrance.

Just as she reached the door to right the misconception that someone else had said something about Graham's affair, the blond woman toppled over a turned table, and the sheriff and deputy attacked the beast of a man that was Graham.

David called out, "Jane, are you all right?"

The woman on the floor blinked. Her movements were slow, but she lifted a hand in a small wave. "I'm fine. I just need a minute. Keep doing what you need to."

"Good," David grunted. "Bastard is fighting us half asleep. Daisy! We need something to calm him down."

Daisy, or as Kat had once known her, Dr. Caroline Pearson, brushed past her with hardly a word. Since Cole's prediction had once again proven right, and Caroline had become Daisy the whore, she hardly spoke to Kat when she returned. Maybe because she was embarrassed, Kat couldn't be sure.

Kat shrugged off the thoughts and turned her attention back to the woman on the floor. She walked up and grinned down at Jane, even though her eyes were closed. "Sure you're fine?" Truth was, she'd feel guilty if the woman was hurt, but Kat hoped she really was all right.

Jane cracked open a bright blue eyes, then blinked them both at Kat's ankles. With a shake of her head, Jane lifted her gaze up to Kat's. A slow chuckle lit her features into a warm smile. "You must be Katherine."

Kat nodded and grinned broader. "You got me. You still didn't answer my question. Are you sure you're fine?"

"A little sore, but I guess it's better than being trapped under that beast."

"Makes you wonder how Linh managed, doesn't it?" Kat held out her hand to help Jane to her feet. "Come on."

Jane took her hand and accepted the help to her feet. After she'd stretched out with a groan, she nodded to Kat. "I'm Jane, by the way."

"Good to meet you. I'm sorry he blamed you. I was the one that blabbed."

"Even if he knew that, he would have blamed me." Jane sighed as Graham was dragged past them, unconscious. She rubbed the back of her neck as she scanned the building. "They just had to rebuild a few months ago, thanks to the renegades. Now this."

"They'll manage. Always do." Kat set her hands on her hips and pursed her lips. Guilt over her part in the chaos nagged at her. "But I guess I should help clean up. It's appropriate penance for causing it."

"You really blabbed?"

"Yes. I found it amusing and shared it with Hammy."

"That was your first mistake."

Kat didn't bother to contain her laughter. She already liked Jane, the woman had a good sense of humor and understood several of the townies already. "Oh, so true. He's a bigger gossip than my sister."

Jane's cough didn't quite cover a giggle. She sighed. "I'm sure your sister had plenty to say about me."

"She sure did. Didn't seem to like you much in general, but was appreciative of your attempt to help once she was in jail."

"Feeling's mutual. We tolerate civility." A blush burned bright on Jane's cheeks. "Not that she's not a good person. She let me stay in the boarding house. She—"

"No need." Kat held up her hand to stem the rambling. If anyone knew the sort of person Martha was, it was Kat. "She's judgmental. A bit of a hypocrite, really. She's my sister, I know. However, that's how I knew I'd like you."

"Oh, really?"

"Really." After all, anyone her sister could work up the venom to dislike, had to be someone Kat would love. She brushed some dust from her bodice. "Well I'd better get to work. See if I can't get some of those lousy drunks to help."

"I'll help."

Kat stopped short in surprise. While she'd heard of Jane's torrid affair with Cole, she also heard they'd parted ways quite certainly, to the point of ignoring each other. "Why?"

Jane didn't meet her gaze, instead bending to right a chair. "I have a sick need to keep helping Cole."

"Oh. We're going to get along just fine, Jane. Just fine."

*To Be*

*Continued...*

In the rest of

# The

# Dominion

# Falls Series

# About the Author

Sarah Cass, author of over twenty novels in 4 series, is devoted to giving her readers well-crafted, emotional stories, with depth to even her secondary characters—to give readers a full world to explore. Stories that explore not only the labyrinths of the heart, but the nightmares of the soul. A RONE finalist, she is also owner and creator of Redefining Perfect. By day, she's a nurse, a mother, wife and cat-mom to 4 mischievous beasts. By night she crafts stories that take her across centuries. From the old west of Dominion Falls, to the small town of Lake Point for the holidays, and even into the paranormal land of Shifters and Magic in The Tribe. She loves hearing from her readers. Visit her at www.authorsarahcass.com

# Other Books in
# The Dominion Falls Series

Changing Tracks
Derailed
Dark Territory
Runaway Train
Home Signal
Red Zone

# Coming Soon in
# The Dominion Falls Series

Dust Raiser
Blizzard Lights
Dead Man's Switch
Bird Cage
A Highball Arrangement
Douse the Glim
Blood
Grave Digger
Bad Order

# Books by Sarah Cass

**The Tribe Series**

The Tribe

The Wolf

The Chief

The Raven

**The Lake Point Series**

Santa, Maybe

Deep-Fried Sweethearts

Stalled Independence

Witch Way

A Thorough Thanksgiving

Eve's New Year

Heartstrings & Hockey Pucks

Luck of the Cowgirl

Stars, Stripes & Motorbikes

Free Falling

Love for Hire

Haunted Hearts

**Stand Alone Novels**

Masked Hearts

Leap

www.ingramcontent.com/pod-product-compliance
Lightning Source LLC
Chambersburg PA
CBHW060154130626
46556CB00006B/2640